Grant pushed Dahlia's head down a second before something exploded...

The truck jerked beneath them. Someone had shot out its tire.

He and Dahlia were on a highway that didn't see much traffic. Which meant this was very carefully planned, and not good for either of them.

The truck's tire rim screeched against concrete, at a bad angle that meant the whole thing could flip if Grant wasn't careful.

He slammed on the brakes, and Dahlia let out a little yelp as the seat belt kept her from slamming into the dash. He ripped the keys out of the ignition. "Keep down," he ordered. He unlocked the glove compartment, then scanned the world around them as he pulled his gun out.

He spotted the shooter in the rearview mirror—up on a ridge and working his way down it. But as far as Grant was concerned, that was the least of his problems. There were three other men moving out from various areas—moving to circle him and Dahlia...

COLD CASE KIDNAPPING

Nicole Helm

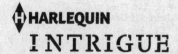

For the reluctant heroes.

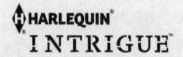

ISBN-13: 978-1-335-59060-2

Cold Case Kidnapping

Copyright © 2023 by Nicole Helm

Recycling programs
for this product may
not exist in your area.

For questions and comments about the quality of this book,
please contact us at CustomerService@Harlequin.com.

Harlequin Enterprises ULC
22 Adelaide St. West, 41st Floor
Toronto, Ontario M5H 4E3, Canada
www.Harlequin.com

Printed in U.S.A.

Nicole Helm grew up with her nose in a book and the dream of one day becoming a writer. Luckily, after a few failed career choices, she gets to follow that dream—writing down-to-earth contemporary romance and romantic suspense. From farmers to cowboys, Midwest to *the* West, Nicole writes stories about people finding themselves and finding love in the process. She lives in Missouri with her husband and two sons, and dreams of someday owning a barn.

Books by Nicole Helm

Harlequin Intrigue

Hudson Sibling Solutions

Cold Case Kidnapping

Covert Cowboy Soldiers

The Lost Hart Triplet
Small Town Vanishing
One Night Standoff
Shot in the Dark
Casing the Copycat
Clandestine Baby

A North Star Novel Series

Summer Stalker
Shot Through the Heart
Mountainside Murder
Cowboy in the Crosshairs
Dodging Bullets in Blue Valley
Undercover Rescue

Visit the Author Profile page at Harlequin.com.

CAST OF CHARACTERS

Grant Hudson—Lead investigator on the Easton case for Hudson Sibling Solutions (HSS), a family-run cold case investigation business operated from the family's ranch. Former marine.

Dahlia Easton—A librarian looking for her missing sister so she hires HSS.

Rose Easton—Dahlia's missing sister, whom she's determined to find and bring home.

Mary Hudson—A Hudson sibling in charge of the administrative work for HSS.

Palmer Hudson—A Hudson sibling working as an investigator for HSS when it's his turn.

Cash Hudson—A Hudson sibling who trains dogs and tries to stay out of HSS business to protect his daughter, Izzy.

Jack Hudson—The oldest Hudson sibling, who founded HSS and also works as sheriff of Sunrise, Wyoming.

Anna Hudson—The youngest Hudson sibling, who investigates for HSS while also working for herself as a private investigator on a variety of cases.

Chapter One

Grant Hudson had been well versed in fear since the age of sixteen when his parents vanished—seemingly into thin air, never to be seen or heard from again. So, as an adult, he'd made fear and uncertainty his life. First, in the military with the Marines and now as a cold case investigator with his siblings.

Privately investigating cold cases didn't involve the same kind of danger he'd seen in Middle Eastern deserts, but the uncertainty, the puzzles and never knowing which step to take was just as much a part of his current life as it had been in the Marines.

And if he focused on seemingly unsolvable cases all day, he didn't have time to think about the nightmares that plagued him.

"Your ten o'clock appointment is here."

Grant looked up from his coffee. His sister was dressed for ranch work but held a file folder that likely had all the information about his new case.

Hudson Sibling Solutions, HSS, was a family

affair. The brainchild of his oldest brother, Jack, and a well-oiled machine in which all six Hudson siblings played a part, just as they all played a part in running the Hudson Ranch that had been in their family for five generations.

They had solved more cases than they hadn't, and Grant considered that a great success. Usually the answers weren't happy endings, but in some strange way, it helped ease the unknowns in their own parents' case.

Grant glanced at the clock as he finished off his coffee. "It's only nine forty-five."

"She's prompt," Mary agreed, handing him the file. "She's in the living room whenever you're ready."

But "whenever you're ready" wasn't part and parcel with what HSS offered.

They didn't make people wait. They didn't shunt people off to small offices and cramped spaces. Usually people trying to get answers on a cold case had spent enough time in police stations, detective offices and all manner of uncomfortable rooms answering the same questions over and over again.

The Hudsons knew that better than anyone— particularly Jack, who'd been the last person to see their parents alive and had been the only legal adult in the family at the time of their disappearance. Jack had been adamant when they began the family investigation business that they offer a different experience for those left behind.

So they met their clients in the homey living room of the Hudson ranch house. They didn't make people wait if they could help it. They treated their clients like guests… The kind of hospitality their mother would have been proud of.

Grant had made himself familiar with today's case prior to this morning, but he skimmed the file Mary had handed off. A missing person, not out of the ordinary for Hudson Sibling Solutions. Dahlia Easton had reported her sister, Rose, missing about thirteen months ago, after her sister had disappeared on a trip to Texas.

Dahlia Easton herself was a librarian from Minnesota. Dahlia was convinced she'd found evidence that placed Rose near Sunrise, Wyoming—which had led her to the HSS.

Ms. Easton hadn't divulged that evidence yet, instead insisting on an in-person meeting to do such. It was Grant's turn to take the lead, so he walked through the hallway that still housed all the framed art his mother had hung once upon a time—various Wyoming landscapes—to the living room.

A redhead sat on the couch, head down and focused on the phone she held. Her long hair curtained her face, and she didn't look up as Grant entered.

He stepped farther into the room and cleared this throat. "Ms. Easton."

The woman looked up from her phone and blinked at him. She didn't move. She sat there as he held out his hand waiting for her to shake it or greet him in some way.

It was a strange thing to see a pretty woman seated on the couch he'd once crowded onto with all his siblings to watch Disney movies. Stranger still to feel the gut kick of attraction.

It made him incredibly uncomfortable when he rarely allowed himself discomfort. He should be thrilled his body could still react to a pretty woman in a perfectly normal way, but he found nothing but a vague sense of unease filling him as she sat there, eyes wide, studying him.

Her hair was a dark red, her eyes a deep tranquil blue on a heart-shaped face that might have been more arresting if she didn't have dark circles under her eyes and her clothes didn't seem to hang off a too-skinny frame. Like many of the clients who came to HSS for help, she wore the physical toll of what she'd been through in obvious ways…enough for even a stranger to notice.

He set those impressions and his own discomfort aside and smiled welcomingly. "Ms. Easton, I'm Grant Hudson. I'll be taking the lead on your case on behalf of HSS. While all six of us work in different facets of investigation, I'll be your point person." He finally dropped his hand since she clearly wasn't going to shake it. "May I?" he said pointing to the armchair situated across from the couch. His father had fallen asleep in that very chair every single movie night.

"You look like a cowboy," she said, her voice sounding raspy from overuse or lack of sleep, presumably.

The corner of his mouth quirked up, a lick of amusement working through him. He supposed a cowboy was quite a sight for someone from Minnesota. "Well, I suppose in a way I am."

"Right. Wyoming. Of course." She shook her head. "I'm sorry. I'm out of sorts."

"No apologies necessary." He settled himself on the chair. She didn't look so much out of sorts as she did exhausted. He set the file down on the coffee table in between them.

"I have all the information Mary collected from you."

"Mary's the woman I talked to on the phone and emailed. I thought she'd…"

"Mary handles the administrative side of things, but I'll be taking the lead on actually investigating. I can get Mary to sit in if you'd feel more comfortable with a woman present?"

"No, it isn't that. I just…" She shook her head. "This is fine."

Grant nodded, then decided what this woman needed was to get some sleep and a good meal in her. "Have you had breakfast?"

"Um." Her eyebrows drew together. "I don't understand what you're..."

"I'd like you to recount everything you know, so we might be here a while. Just making sure you're up for it."

"Oh, I'm not much for breakfast."

He'd figured as much. He pulled his phone out of his pocket and sent a quick text to Mary. He wouldn't push the subject, but he wasn't about to let Dahlia keel over either. He slid the phone back in his pocket.

"I've got your file here. All about your sister's trip to Texas. The credit card reports, cell phone records. Everything you gave us. But you said you had reason to believe she ended up here in Wyoming."

"Yes," Dahlia agreed, putting her own phone into a bag that sat next to her. "Everything the police uncovered happened in Texas," Dahlia said. "But she just...disappeared into thin air, as far as anyone can tell me, but obviously that isn't true. People can't just disappear."

But they did. All the time. There were a lot of ways to make sure a person was never found. More than even Grant could probably fathom, and he could fathom a lot. Which was why he focused on one individual case at a time. "So, there's no evidence she ever left Texas?"

"She took one of those DNA tests, and it matched her with some people in Texas," Dahlia said earnestly, avoiding the direct question. "She was supposed to go to Texas and meet them. She never made it to the people—at least the police there didn't think so. When all the clues dried up, I decided to look at Rose's research. The genealogy stuff that prompted her to take the DNA test. I researched everything she had, and it led me to a secret offshoot of the Texas family that wound up in Truth, Wyoming."

Grant tried not to frown. Because, no, there wasn't proof Rose Easton had left Texas, and also because no one in Sunrise particularly cared to think about Truth, Wyoming. "Ah" was all he said.

"It's a cult."

"It was a cult," Grant replied. "The Feds wiped them out before I was born." Still, people tried to stir up all the Order of Truth nonsense every few years. But there was no evidence that the cult had done anything but die out after the federal raid in 1978.

"Doesn't everything gone come around back again?" Dahlia asked, nervous energy pumping off her. "And if this line of our family was involved then, doesn't it mean they could be involved now?"

Grant studied the woman. She looked tired and brittle. It didn't diminish her beauty, just gave it a fragile hue. Fragile didn't cut it in these types of situations, but here she was. Still standing. Still searching.

She was resting all her hopes on the wrong thing if she was looking into the Order of Truth, but she believed it. She was clearly holding on to this tiny thread for dear life. So Grant smiled kindly. "Let's see your evidence."

HE DIDN'T BELIEVE HER. No different than any of the police officers and detectives back home or in Texas. Once Dahlia uttered the word *cult*—especially one that had been famously wiped out—people stopped listening.

Grant Hudson was no different, except he was placating her by asking for her evidence. Dahlia didn't know if that was more insulting than waving her off or not. Honestly, she was too tired to figure out how she felt about much of anything.

She'd driven almost eighteen hours from Minneapolis to Sunrise in two days and had barely slept last night in the nice little cabin she'd rented. She was too anxious and tangled up about this strange connection. Too amped at the thought of *hope* after so long.

"I think you probably have all the evidence you care about," Dahlia said, trying to keep her tone even. "I know investigators are obsessed with facts, but facts haven't helped me. Sometimes you have to tie some ideas together to find the facts."

Grant studied her. It had been a silly thing to

say, that he looked like a cowboy, but it was simply true. It wasn't just the drawl, it was something about the way he walked. There were the cowboy boots of course, and the Western decor all around them, but something in the square jaw or slightly crooked nose made her think of the Wild West. The way he hadn't fully smiled, but his mouth had *curved* in a slow move that had left her scrambling for words.

"We are investigators, and we do have to work in the truth," Grant said, still using that kind veneer to his words, though Dahlia sensed an irritation simmering below them. "But I think you'll find we're not like the police departments you've dealt with. I'll admit, I think the cult is the wrong tree to bark up, but if you give me reason to change my mind, I'll bark away."

The tall slender woman who'd let her in the house entered the room pushing a cart. She wore adorable cowboy boots with colorful flowers on them and Dahlia had no doubt when she spoke, it would be tinged with that same smooth Western drawl Grant had.

It was easy to see the two were related even if Grant was tall and broad and...*built*.

There was something in the eyes, in the way they moved. Dahlia didn't have the words for it, just that they functioned like a unit. One that had been in each other's pockets their whole lives.

People had never been able to tell that about her

and Rose, aside from being named for flowers. It took getting to know them, together, to see the way they had learned how to deal with each other and their parents. The rhythm of being a sibling.

Dahlia had been turned into an only child now, and she didn't know how to function in that space. Not with her parents, who had given up on Rose when the police had. Not with her friends, all of whom were more Rose's friends than hers and who wanted to be involved in a tragedy and their grief more than they wanted answers.

Only Dahlia couldn't let it go. Couldn't hold on to her old life in this new world where her sister didn't exist.

Not dead. Not gone. She didn't *exist*.

"I told you I'm not a breakfast eater," Dahlia said sharply and unkindly. She might have felt bad about that, felt her grandmother's disapproval from half a country away, but she was tired of caring what everyone else felt.

Grant apparently felt unbothered by her snap. "So consider it lunch." He looked at his sister. "Thanks, Mary."

She nodded, smiled at Dahlia, then left. Grant immediately took a plate and began to arrange things on it. Dahlia figured he'd shove it at her, and she had all sorts of reasons to tell him to shove it down his own throat.

Instead, he set it next to the file folder. Picking a grape and popping it into his own mouth before pouring himself some coffee.

Dahlia knew she'd lost too much weight. She understood she didn't sleep well enough, and her health was suffering because of it. She'd seen a therapist to help her come to terms with Rose's disappearance.

But no amount of self-awareness or therapy could stop her from this driving need to find the truth.

She didn't know if Rose was still alive. She was prepared—or tried to prepare herself—for the ugly truths that could be awaiting her. Namely, that Rose was dead and had been all this time. Her sweet, vibrant sister. Murdered and discarded.

It wasn't just possible, it was likely, and yet Dahlia had to know. She couldn't rest, not really, until she had the truth.

And if you never find it?

She simply didn't know. So she'd keep going until something changed.

Grant continued to eat as he flipped through papers that were presumably the reports and information she'd emailed to Mary.

Dahlia wasn't hungry, but she hadn't been for probably the entire past year. Still, food was fuel, and this food was free. She could hardly sidestep that when her entire life savings was being poured into hiring Hudson Sibling Solutions and staying in Wyoming until the mystery was solved.

She finally forced herself to pick a few pieces of fruit and a hard-boiled egg and put them on a plate. She'd been guzzling coffee for days, so she went for the bottle of water instead.

"Tell me why you decided to come all the way out here." He said it silky smooth, and whether it was the drawl or his demeanor, he made it sound like a gentle request.

She knew it was an order though. And she knew he'd ignore it like everyone else had. It was too big of a leap to take, and yet…

"Rose found out our great-grandfather was married before he married our great-grandmother. And he had a son from this first marriage. A man named Eugene Green."

Grant's expression didn't move, but something in the air around them did. Likely because he knew Eugene Green to be the founder of the Order of Truth.

"That's not exactly a close relation, is it? Something like a half great-great-uncle. If that."

"If that," Dahlia agreed. Her stomach turned, but still she forced herself to eat a grape. Drink some of the water. "But it was in Rose's notes."

Grant flipped through the papers again. "What notes?"

Dahlia moved for her bag and pulled out the thick binder she'd been carting around. "After the police decided it was a cold case, they returned her computer to me. I printed off everything she'd collected about our family history. *That's* what took her to Texas. She had a binder just like this. With more originals, but she scanned and labeled everything. So I recreated it. The Wyoming branch and Texas branch of the family are one and the same. It connects."

Grant eyed the binder. "Ms. Easton…"

"I know. You don't believe me. No one does. That's okay." She hadn't come all this way just for someone to believe her. "And you can hardly look through it all. But there is this." She pulled out the piece of paper she'd been keeping in the front pocket of the binder. "The picture on the top is from security footage of the gas station in Texas where Rose was last spotted. That's Rose," she said pointing to her sister. "No one can identify the man with her, but he looks an awfully lot like the picture on the bottom. A picture of Eugene Green from my sister's notes."

Grant didn't even flick a glance at the picture. "Eugene Green is dead."

"Yes, but not everyone who might look like him is."

Grant seemed to consider this, but then people—law enforcements, investigators, even friends—always did. At first. "Can I keep this?"

Dahlia nodded. She had digital copies of everything. She wasn't taking any chances. If HSS took all her information and lost it, discarded it or ignored it, she'd always have her own copies to keep her going.

"Did you have anything else that might tie Rose to Truth or Wyoming?" Grant asked.

No, she hadn't come here thinking HSS would believe her, but she'd…hoped. She couldn't seem to stop herself from hoping. "No, not exactly."

"Can I ask why you couldn't have told us this over the phone?"

Dahlia looked at the picture. Every police officer she'd talked to about it told her she was grasping at straws. That the Order of Truth was gone, and all the Greens had long since left the Truth area. That the man in the picture wasn't *with* Rose. He was just getting gas at the pump next to her.

"I'm not sure I could explain it in a way that would make any sense to you, but I needed to come here."

Grant nodded. "Well, I'll look into this. Is there anything else?"

Dahlia shoved her binder, sans security picture, back in her bag and then stood. He was dismissing her now that he understood her evidence was circumstantial—according to the police.

She was disappointed. She could admit that to herself. She'd expected or hoped for a miracle. Even as she'd told herself they wouldn't care any more than anyone else had, there'd been a seed of hope this family solving cold cases might believe her.

She should end this. The Hudsons weren't going to do any more than the police had, and she was going to run out of money eventually. "If you don't have anything new in a week, I suppose that will be that."

His eyebrows rose as he stood. "A week isn't much time to solve a cold case."

"I don't need it solved. I just need some forward movement to prove I'm paying for something tangible. If you can prove to me the Order of Truth has nothing to do with this—irrefutably—that'll be enough."

He seemed to consider this, then gave her a nod. "You're staying at the Meadowlark Cabin?" Grant asked as he motioned her to follow him.

Dahlia nodded as she retraced her footsteps through the big stone-floored foyer to the large front door with its stained glass sidelights. Mountains and stars.

"How long are you planning on staying?"

Dahlia looked away from the glass mountains to Grant's austere face. "As long as it takes."

Again, his expression didn't quite move, but she got the distinct feeling he didn't approve. Still, he said nothing, just opened the front door.

"I'll be in touch," he said.

She forced herself to smile and shake his outstretched hand.

Just because he'd be in touch didn't mean she was going to go hole herself in her room at her rented cabin in Sunrise. No.

She planned on doing some investigating of her own. She'd come here hoping the Hudsons could help, sure, but she'd known what she really needed to do.

Help herself.

Chapter Two

"Did you know about this?"

Mary looked down from where she was situated on her horse. She adjusted the reins in her hands and then studied the paper Grant held. Mary frowned. "Is that Eugene Green?"

"Your new client seems to think he's involved."

Her frown deepened. "Did you mention that he died like fifty years ago?"

"I did. I also mentioned the Feds wiped out the Order of Truth in the seventies. You're supposed to do a better job of weeding out the pointless cases."

Mary's frown turned into a blank look she'd perfected. People who didn't know her might consider it a nonreaction, but Grant was her brother. He knew better. And he knew he'd pay for it later. But his irritation with cult nonsense overrode self-preservation at the moment.

"Did she seem *pointless* to you?" Mary asked, her voice calm if icy.

"Not until she pulled out this picture."

"So she's misdirected. Following the wrong lead. People do that kind of thing. Even us." Mary's horse puffed out a breath, energy pumping off the large animal. It was ready for a run, for some work.

But Mary kept the horse still, waiting for Grant to respond in some way.

There were a million dead ends when it came to investigating cold cases. A lot of retracing steps and looking at the same evidence over and over again, trying to find a different angle or shed a new light. And, yes, sometimes an investigator went down the wrong path. More than once.

Even him.

Still, Grant wanted nothing to do with Truth. He'd never found the cult stories interesting the way some people did. Maybe it was the family connection, even if it didn't connect to him. Because like Dahlia and Rose Easton, he had broken branches of a family tree too.

Grant had always felt in line with his mother's track of thinking on the matter. Best not to dwell on it. Best to leave it alone.

Besides, the ghost town of Truth had never done anything except give him a bad feeling—one he now recognized as the same bad feeling he'd gotten in the Marines before something had gone FUBAR.

But their client thought Truth had something to do with her case, and unless Grant's people skills were rusty, he was willing to bet Dahlia Easton wouldn't let that angle go without some proof. So, he had to prove to her she was on the wrong path, and then maybe he could help her find the right one.

"I'm taking one of the dogs," Grant muttered.

"Better clear it with Cash," Mary replied, and she didn't smile exactly, but Grant could read the smug satisfaction all the same. "And make sure to use the business credit card for gas."

Grant rolled his eyes. "I'm not Palmer."

"You're all men, and men are constantly forgetting important details. At least the men I know."

Before he could respond to that, Mary urged her horse forward, and it more than willingly obliged, leaving Grant standing in a cloud of dust.

Grant considered the horse stables. He could take one over. Cash's dog barn was on the other side of the property, as was the cabin where he lived with his eleven-year-old. Izzy would be at school, which meant Cash would likely be training his dogs. Cash trained all sorts of dogs, search and rescue, detection, even some service dogs.

But if Grant took a horse over, he'd have to come back and deal with the aftercare. He wanted this trip done with ASAP. So he got his truck and drove the dusty path from the main part of the ranch to Cash's little corner of it.

It was a sunny fall day, warm enough, but the air would go cold the minute the sun started dipping toward the horizon. The sky was a dark blue, and the land of the Hudson Ranch stretched out around him in rolling hills and long plains that led to those timeless craggy mountains in the distance. No matter what he'd seen out there in the world, Sunrise and this ranch had always been home to the most beautiful sky in the whole world.

He'd always known he'd come back here. The military had been a side trip. To get out of Jack's hair. Assuage some of the restlessness inside of him. See the world. Fight for his country. *Do* something outside of Sunrise and everyone who knew him and defined him by his tragedy.

But he'd always known when that side trip was over, he'd be back here. Working the same land his great-great-great-grandfather had.

Grant came to a stop next to the dog barn, a squat red building where Cash housed all his dogs. Cash himself stood outside in front of a line of dogs. If he'd been in the mood for it, Grant might have found some amusement in how much the sight reminded him of soldiers standing at attention awaiting their orders.

Grant parked and got out, then walked toward his brother as Cash made a hand signal. The dogs all sat in unison. Another hand movement, they all laid down.

Only once Cash was satisfied every dog had

its stomach on the ground did he turn to Grant. "What's up?"

"I need a dog for a job. Few hours tops. Nothing special. More company than anything." Grant had no desire to head out to that eerie place alone.

Cash nodded, studied his pack. "Willie." He gave a sharp whistle, and a brown-and-white shepherd got up and trotted over to them. "Don't feed him scraps."

"You're always telling me that."

"Yeah, and you're always ignoring me."

Grant chuckled. True enough. He planned to continue to do so. Who could resist those soulful canine eyes just begging for a treat?

Cash made some more of his hand gestures and different sounding whistles, and Willie bounded up into Grant's truck.

"This about the Easton missing person case?" Cash asked, closing the truck door behind the dog.

"Yeah. How'd you know that? I thought you were keeping your nose out of cases."

"I try, but between Anna and Palmer's big mouths I end up knowing far more than I want to." Cash glanced back at the house. Though Grant knew Izzy was at school, he also knew that's who his brother was thinking about.

Cash would have taken a more active role in cases if he wasn't worried about his daughter's safety or his own as a single father. Which was why, even though he tried to keep his nose out of things, he'd inevitably ask…

"So, what was the Wyoming connection?"

"Tenuous at best," Grant replied. He didn't want to get into it, but no doubt Cash would hear about it one way or another. The only way to prove it didn't bother him was to be the one to tell him. "She thinks it connects to Truth."

It was Cash's turn to chuckle. "Isn't it funny how the one of us the most afraid of Truth got picked for lead investigator on a case that connects to it?"

"The case doesn't connect to Truth. The Easton woman just thinks it does. I'm headed there to prove to her she's wrong." He knew he should leave it at that, but Cash always knew how to needle him into giving up more information than he cared to. "I'm hardly afraid."

"Fifteen-year-old Grant sure was."

"Yeah, well unless you and Palmer have concocted yet another plan to attempt to scare the—"

"Oh, it wasn't an attempt. We scared the living daylights out of you."

Grant rolled his eyes. "I went to war, Cash. I'm not afraid of Truth, Wyoming. Or you and Palmer for that matter," Grant muttered, adjusting his cowboy hat on his head. He got into his truck, ignoring his brother's mocking laughter.

Truth be told—a fact he'd never admit to his brothers—he'd rather be back in the Marines than spend the next few days in Truth, but he'd learned a long time ago, a man didn't always get what he'd rather.

TRUTH, WYOMING, was a ghost town. Dahlia wasn't surprised. Everything she'd read about it told her that after the federal raid had ended in three dead FBI agents, ten dead cult members and the rest of the adults jailed for life, no one had wanted anything to do with the town except the occasional tourist to gawk at the scene of tragedy.

But no one stayed. No one built inappropriate tourist attractions. It had been the site of something gruesome that no one understood. A fascination, surely, but not one to spend more than a few hours in.

So, no, Dahlia wasn't surprised the buildings were empty or that here on the rock cropping she'd climbed to look down at the town, the land stretched out, gray and brown and deserted and what she figured most would find unappealing.

What did surprise her was the way the ethereal beauty of the area struck her someplace deep inside. It was nothing like home. No green, no sparkling lakes, no fall colors. The land stretched out in all directions, the same grayish color, routinely interrupted by strange rock formations—some skinny and jagged reaching for the sky. Some big fat columns of earth. But it didn't feel like some alien planet. It felt alive and vibrant.

It felt...*right*. As if she belonged down there, walking the length of the abandoned street. She didn't understand the feeling at all. It made her want to cry. Inexplicably.

You're just exhausted, she told herself as she climbed back down the rock. What had she expected to find here? Signs of her sister? Or any civilization? She was exhausted and it was affecting her decision making.

But she walked down what had once been Main Street, and she knew she should feel out of place. Creeped out, maybe, but there was only a thrumming curiosity that had her poking her head into doors. She didn't know what she was looking for or what she was hoping to prove. She was just following instinct...or her gut...or something.

The same something that had pushed her to leave her life behind and come here to begin with. Everything had frozen in place once Rose had disappeared. Dahlia didn't know how to unfreeze it without figuring out...something. *Something.*

She walked into a building that had clearly once been a restaurant of some kind. A few tables were still scattered around the main room, a counter ran along the far wall, with an empty display case that looked like it might have once been filled with baked goods.

Dust and grime stuck to every surface. No one had been here lately. That was clear. Even if they had, why would they leave evidence of it? And what would she do if she found it?

She should have gone back to her rental cabin and slept. This was a waste of time. She should be searching the Green family and their connection to hers, not some Wyoming ghost town.

Maybe her parents were right. She couldn't think straight. She should commit herself until she could again. But Dahlia knew she hadn't had any sort of mental break. Maybe she had let emotions affect her decision-making, but she…

She had to see this through. The right way though. Taking care of herself had to start being a priority.

She stepped out of the abandoned building and then stopped abruptly. A shudder moved through her. That odd peace she didn't understand evaporated. Replaced by the feeling of being watched.

She swallowed at the bubble of fear. Her eyes darted from side to side as she stood rooted to the spot. She didn't see anything out of the ordinary. She held her breath and listened, trying to discern something beyond the gentle rustle of the wind.

A faint high-pitched sound cut the silence, then was hushed by a quiet command. Dahlia told herself to move, but fear kept her frozen in the doorway. *Run! Hide! Scream!*

She did none of those things. She couldn't. Apparently in a flight-or-fight response situation, Dahlia went with neither.

A soft yip—like from a dog—echoed through the air, and then a large brown-and-white dog appeared around a corner. Relief coursed through her. She nearly sagged against the doorway behind her. Just a dog. Just a—

"Willie. Sit."

It was a man's voice. Sharp and commanding. And the dog immediately plopped its butt on the dusty ground a few yards away. She didn't see the man, but something about actually hearing a voice, or maybe the dog itself, prompted Dahlia into action. She scurried back into the building, crouching behind the wall so that no one could see her from outside.

She pressed her back against the wall. She tried to hold her breath but realized belatedly that wouldn't be sustainable.

How would she know when the man was gone? Would the dog sniff her out? Why was she acting like she needed to hide when she had just as much right to be here as anyone else? As far as she could tell, the land was public property and...

She heard the dog, the faint panting noises, the padding of paws closer and closer and closer until...

"Closing your eyes doesn't stop the bad guy from coming, Ms. Easton."

Dahlia blinked her eyes open and looked up at the tall shadow of a man who stood in the doorway. She hadn't realized she'd screwed her eyes shut in some childish instinct.

Embarrassment washed over her more than fear when she recognized the man.

She frowned at Grant Hudson's disapproving face. "What are you doing here?"

"Shouldn't that be my line?"

She hadn't expected…this. At all. He'd been so dismissive. "You're investigating."

"I said I would."

"I didn't think you'd actually look into Truth."

"You said you needed proof it didn't connect." He held out a hand, and it took Dahlia quite a few ticking seconds to realize he was offering to help her to her feet. She found she didn't want to slide her hand in his but couldn't say why. So she went against instinct and took it.

Firm and callused, he grasped her hand and leveraged her to her feet. The minute she was upright and steady, he immediately let her hand go. He strode back out to the street without another word.

Dahlia didn't know what else to do but follow, like the dog.

"Is this proof enough?" he asked, waving to the empty town around them.

Dahlia followed the path of his hand with her gaze. Even knowing she hadn't been watched but instead was running into the investigator she hired, something had changed. She didn't feel that sense of belonging anymore. Only fore-boding.

"Proof that she isn't in Truth right this moment. But that's about it."

Grant sighed. "Ms. Easton, you should under-stand—"

"I know. I'm very well aware she could be dead." People didn't seem to understand that hope didn't mean she was ignoring the very real possibility her sister had been murdered. That thought plagued her, haunted her, just as much as that tiny sliver of hope that Rose was alive somewhere did. That's why she needed the truth.

The dog made another whining noise. Grant looked down at the animal with a faint line of confusion on his brow. "Go," he offered.

The dog took off down the empty street, and Grant followed him, so Dahlia followed Grant. The dog led them down an alley between two buildings that had been enveloped by some kind of winding vine. It was a narrow alley, and even with the bright sunshine overhead the area was shadowed and dark. Dahlia shivered at the cooler temperature here, looking over her shoulder as goose bumps popped up along her arms.

When she looked forward again, Grant had stopped and was frowning in the same direction she'd been looking. But he shook his head and pressed forward through the alley.

Once on the other side, Dahlia was surprised

and confused to find a kind of walled courtyard. Thick, tall stone walls were built along the perimeter—the alley apparently the only way in or out. There was no roof, only the bright blue sky, and there was nothing of note in the courtyard. Just a square of dusty ground and a few patches of grass or brush.

But the dog continued yapping, and as Grant strode over to the corner where it stood, Dahlia's unease intensified. She moved slowly toward where Grant was crouched. He was staring at a small piece of something on the ground.

"What is it?"

"Casing," he replied somewhat absently.

"What does that mean?"

"Someone shot a gun here. And not that long ago." Grant studied the small object, frowning. "Could have been someone target-shooting. It could be a lot of things." He stood, but there was something…off. He held himself differently now. The frown on his face was more serious.

"So, why do you look so…perplexed?"

He looked up, studying their surroundings with a cold detachment that made her aware she was alone with a virtual stranger in a very isolated landscape. Stuck in this little courtyard, as no doubt Grant could block off the one exit before she could make it out.

When his eyes met hers, they were dark and not at all comforting. "Let's get you back to town."

Chapter Three

Something wasn't right. Grant didn't believe it had anything to do with Truth. But it definitely had something to do with the woman driving in front of him.

Grant glanced in his rearview mirror. He'd half expected someone to follow them out of Truth. Half expected *something* to happen, though he couldn't have said what.

He wished he'd had time to investigate, but instinct told him to get Dahlia out of there, and he was still enough of a soldier to follow his instincts.

She hadn't argued. Oh, she'd looked at him a bit like he might be the Devil sent to take her to hell, but she'd done as he said. Walked back to her car, gotten in, then waited for him to bring his truck around so he could follow her back to Sunrise.

He glanced at the rearview again. He couldn't shake the feeling someone had been watching them. He hadn't seen any evidence of that. It was just a feeling.

But added to the lone shell casing, they needed to do a full-blown search of Truth. Much as he was loath to admit it.

It could be unrelated. People went to Truth sometimes. High school kids went out on a dare. Yahoos driven by stories on the internet went out to do whatever rituals they thought might make something happen. That casing could mean anything.

But there'd been a mark on the wall—mostly scrubbed off—that made Grant suspicious *something* was going on in Truth even if it had nothing to do with the missing Easton sister. *Or* the cult.

But he had to get Dahlia tucked away before he could deal with that. She pulled her car off the highway. Surprisingly not a rental, but a compact sedan registered to Dahlia Easton of Minneapolis, Minnesota.

He'd called Zadie, an old family friend now with the sheriff's department, to get him that information. Taking her own car rather than flying or even renting for a few weeks spoke of something longer than a brief trip to check things out.

But Dahlia herself wasn't the case. The missing sister was. And now, for Grant, the case included figuring out what was going on in Truth.

It was a short drive off the highway to the cabin Dahlia was renting. Just inside Sunrise's borders, it was secluded—a pretty little cabin in a pretty little spot.

But she'd do better somewhere with a little bit more foot traffic. Grant didn't believe anywhere was don't-lock-your-doors safe, but Sunrise was about as close as a person could get. She should be closer to people who would, if nothing else, notice if something fishy went on. Then the gossip chain would let the Hudsons know before anything bad happened.

Dahlia got out of her car, and she gripped her bag so hard her knuckles were white. She stayed close to her car as Grant got out of his truck. "You didn't have to follow me here."

She wasn't comfortable with him, and he understood. He wished he could give her more space, but something was off. The safety of a client came before their comfort.

Still, Grant whistled for Willie to get out of the car. She seemed to relax a little bit around the dog.

"I'm just going to have a look around," he said, trying to sound casual as Willie ambled over to sit next to her.

She looked at the dog. Then him. "Look around what?"

"The cabin."

She shook her head. "Why on earth would you do that?"

"Ms. Easton, did you get the sense you were all alone when you were in Truth?"

"Yes. Yes, it was peaceful actually. Until you came along." She lifted her chin. She might be exhausted, maybe even a little fragile, but she had some fighting spirit in there.

"And what happened when I came along?"

She shook her head. "I don't know. I guess I just…felt your presence or whatever. Not in a woo-woo way. I heard the dog. I…" She trailed off, frowning, but she didn't continue.

He didn't know who might be following her. Who might be hanging around Truth. But he knew there was something off, and he had to wonder if it was something she'd brought with her from Minnesota.

"Would anyone have followed you here? To Sunrise?"

"From Minnesota?"

"Maybe you hired a private investigator? Or there's a family member worried about you? Anyone who might not have wanted you to come here alone."

She blinked, shaking her head. But he knew that was a knee-jerk response. She really needed to consider the possibilities. Maybe she would after he was gone. "I'm just going to do a quick perimeter check. You stay put."

"I—"

He didn't give her a chance to argue. He strode

off, the stay-put order being not just for her but Willie as well.

He didn't expect to find anything. Once he got Dahlia situated, he'd head back to Truth, maybe with Palmer and Anna, and go over the things he'd seen, but he had to make sure all was good here first.

He walked around the side of the cabin. The backyard was a small patch of green. Trees created a kind of frame, and Ursula—the lady who kept the cabin—had colorful blooms in pots all over the back porch.

He studied the windows. There were blinds on them, but they weren't drawn. Right now it was too sunny to get a good look inside, but at night with the lights on, anyone would be able to see what Dahlia was doing.

Grant studied the small backyard, walked the perimeter of it and almost passed the small indentation in the scrubby grass. But then there was another one, where grass met a dusty patch of dirt. And then another—this one, clearly a footprint. Too big to be Dahlia's, or Ursula's for that matter.

Lawn care? Ursula's son? Grant studied each footprint, following its progress toward the house, crossing every potential culprit off the list. Ursula's son lived in Houston and hadn't visited since Christmas. God knew she told everyone who listened that little complaint. Ursula didn't hire out lawn services. She believed in handling things at her rental properties herself.

Grant came to a stop at the cabin. The footprints led right up to the structure on the side. There was a window right in front of him, and if he shaded his eyes to look inside, he could tell it was a bedroom.

Dahlia's bedroom.

Dread curled in his gut. Much like back in Truth, it could be a lot of things. Some Peeping Tom, a burglar, either potentially unrelated to Dahlia.

But they were problems, related or not.

Unfortunately, Grant was struggling to believe all this didn't connect. The timing was too suspect. Everything too…centered around her.

He finished his perimeter check, debating whether to tell Dahlia about the prints. Maybe he could just convince her to go home. Not mention…anything.

A frustrating line of thought. It wasn't his job to protect her feelings or assuage her fears. It was his job to get answers.

He made it back around to the front. She sat on the porch stair scratching Willie behind his ears. She looked up at Grant as he approached, her enjoyment of the dog going cold as their eyes met.

She stood.

Grant thought there was probably a gentle way to put it, but he didn't have it in him to find out.

Not when her hair glittered in the sun, and those blue eyes looked at him with such distrust, made worse by the dark circles under her eyes.

"There are footprints leading up to that back window that looks into your bedroom."

"Footprints," she echoed.

"Not yours."

Her eyebrows furrowed, and she looked back at the cabin, then the world around them. "It could be the…the owner. The cleaning service. It could be…"

Grant wished he could agree, but he knew everyone who would have been walking around the cabin, and none of them had a size twelve military-style boot.

"Dahlia, I think you might be in danger."

GRANT'S WORDS DIDN'T make sense. Not when applied to her. So Dahlia laughed. It seemed the only possible reaction. "I'm not in any danger."

"Someone is watching you. If you don't think it could be someone looking out for you, it's someone who wants something else from you."

"I wasn't being followed. No one followed me."

"You're certain?"

But of course she wasn't. Not when he'd introduced the possibility she was in danger. Something had happened to Rose. Didn't that mean something could happen to her? All because Rose had started digging into the past. And then Dahlia had in order to find Rose. "How can I be certain of anything?"

Something on his face…softened. She certainly wouldn't call his expression kind or his demeanor gentle, but her words seemed to affect him. Some way.

"I don't think it's safe for you to stay here until we figure this out."

Dahlia looked behind her at the pretty little cabin. *Someone is watching you.* "Where would I go?" she said, though she hadn't precisely meant to say it out loud—certainly not as a question geared toward him.

"Why don't you grab your things and come to the ranch for a bit? We'll figure everything out."

"But…you're strangers."

He nodded. "Ones you hired to find your sister."

"Yes, to solve a cold case. Not to…protect me or whatever this is."

Any hint of that earlier softness hardened again. "Ms. Easton—"

"Oh, don't drawl 'Ms. Easton' at me. My name is Dahlia. I don't understand why you think I'm in danger. I don't understand—" she flung her arms up in the air "—any of this."

"Neither do I. That's why I think it'd be smart if you came to the ranch so we can go over your case piece by piece. Determine if there's a real threat."

"What's the other option?"

"Coincidence."

Dahlia huffed out a breath. "None of this feels like a coincidence."

"No, it doesn't. I believe that's my point. Still, we can't be sure until we investigate. Now, if you'd rather stay here—alone, unprotected and isolated—it's a free country. If you'd like to use the full services of HSS, you can pack up your things and follow me back to the ranch."

"I don't care for ultimatums."

"I don't care for interfering clients, but here we are."

When she glared at him, he winced a little. She wasn't sure why. Surely, he was being honest. He didn't seem like the kind of man who felt bad about a little honesty.

But he let out a sigh. "I apologize. You're free to do as you wish, Ms. Easton—*Dahlia*. I'm inviting you to the Hudson Ranch while we analyze the potential threat to you, but if you don't feel comfortable, you certainly can make your own decisions."

His businesslike voice meant to appease her was far worse than him calling her an interfering client.

"You could also go home. Trust us to—"

"No." Going home wasn't an option. Not until she had answers.

"Somehow I figured," he muttered, clearly disapproving of that response. "So? Stay or go?"

She needed more time to think. She needed sleep. She needed…help. That was why she'd come here. That was why she was planning on spending every last cent on finding Rose. Grant had been dismissive of her belief there was a cult connection, but he'd gone to Truth. Right away. He'd investigated.

It was more than anyone else had done.

"I just…" She shook her head and swallowed the words back down. Grant wasn't her friend or her confidant. He was her employee. A partner at best. He didn't need to hear about the emotional circles her brain was running in. "It shouldn't take me too long to pack."

He nodded firmly. "Good. I'll wait in the truck."

She nodded, grateful he wasn't trying to enter the cabin. He'd give her space, if not the opportunity to really figure this out.

She stepped inside the cabin. She hadn't had time to appreciate or enjoy it. Now it was tainted by the knowledge someone had been… In Grant's theory, someone had been watching her through her bedroom window.

She stepped into said bedroom and looked at the big window that overlooked the backyard. Pretty. Peaceful. And someone had allegedly been standing right there. Watching her.

And she'd been clueless. She shuddered against the bolt of fear and unease, then turned to grab her things.

"I can't believe I'm doing this," she muttered to herself. It was insanity. A scam. Maybe she was about to meet her end just as Rose had. Because she was pretty sure on the Hudson Ranch she *could* just disappear. Still, she shoved the few belongings she'd taken out back into her suitcase.

Maybe she *should* go home. Maybe—

Grant was there—suddenly, silently. Like he could simply will himself to appear in her doorway without making any noise.

"Stay here. Lock the door. And whatever you do, don't open it up for anyone." Before she could say anything, he was gone, practically like he'd vanished. But not before she'd watched a gun appear in his hand like magic.

She stood there, suitcase in hand, and then the dog from before padded into the room. He plopped himself right in front of her like he was some kind of guard dog.

It was now clear in a way it hadn't been this whole time.

Dahlia had no idea what she'd gotten herself into.

Chapter Four

Grant moved back outside, hand on his weapon as he scanned the world around the little cabin.

Someone was out there. Not just *had* been out there, but was there right now. Watching. Maybe waiting.

He wasn't about to leave—with or without Dahlia—knowing someone might follow. Maybe Dahlia wasn't in immediate danger, because someone had been watching her for some time and nothing had happened, but there were no good reasons for being watched.

Grant took a second to look back at the cabin, grateful Dahlia hadn't followed and Willie had obeyed the order to stay put. Then Grant moved forward. He'd had that watched feeling when he'd been waiting in the truck, but that wouldn't have been enough for him to act.

Sometimes a soldier didn't fully leave behind that watched feeling. But he'd seen the flash of something in his rearview mirror. Just at the curve of the road. He wasn't going to go straight for it though. He was more tactical than that.

He didn't follow the length of the road, he moved through the yard, using the truck as a kind of cover, hoping to move around enough to get a different angle at the road and see beyond the curve without who or whatever he'd seen knowing.

He held his gun and moved silently and quickly, eyes trained on where he'd first seen the flash of something. As he moved up the slight rise of land at the edge of the yard, he saw it again.

A figure darting too quickly out of sight to tell much about. It could have been a man or a woman. No sense of coloring. Just a shadow—human—then gone.

Grant ran after it, determined to get some clue as to who was watching his client. He pushed away thoughts of strange twists of fate bringing him a case that connected to Truth and all he struggled to forget. He let the mechanics of the all-out run block all those thoughts. There was only one target: whoever was watching them.

But the figure had too much of a head start, and as he came to the curve of the road, he knew going any farther would leave Dahlia alone and too far out of his reach to help if someone else was involved or the runner doubled back.

Grant came to a stop, scanning the landscape. He scowled, and after one last look around and another minute to return his breathing to normal, he turned and walked back to the cabin. He kept his instincts honed to the world around him, but he knew in his gut whoever had been there was long gone.

It ate him up that he couldn't follow, but he'd need to get Ms. Easton somewhere safe first.

There was more to this whole thing than that woman had let on. Well, he'd give her the benefit of the doubt. Maybe she didn't know what she'd gotten herself into. Sometimes that happened, especially with cold cases that weren't quite as cold as people thought.

It did not ease his frustration any. He returned to the cabin, tested the door. She'd followed his instructions and locked it. At least she could follow directions sometimes.

He knocked and waited for her to answer. When she pulled the door open, Willie was still right next to her.

Grant crouched and gave the dog a scratch behind the ears. "Good dog," he murmured, then stood and studied Ms. Easton.

She was looking a little rough around the edges. He had enough sisters to know not to say that out loud. "I saw someone, probably whoever's been watching you, but unfortunately they were too far away to pursue safely. I think it's all the more reason for you to come stay at the ranch."

"Why would someone be watching me?"

He'd also worked with enough clients to know not to give them—particularly the nervous ones—all the possibilities. "Hard to say. We'll figure it out. Let's head on back to the ranch. Why don't I drive you?"

"I have a car." She gestured helplessly at it.

"I know. Let's just leave it here for the time being. A little misdirection."

"Misdirection," she echoed.

She was in some kind of shock maybe. He moved around her and grabbed the suitcase she'd had clutched in her hands when he'd first come in. "Come on," he said, gesturing her forward and then striding through the front door as if he had no doubt she'd follow.

But he did actually have a few doubts. He made it to the truck before he allowed himself to look over his shoulder. She was following, Willie at her side, but clearly not convinced this was the best course of action.

He got in the driver's seat and texted his sisters to get a room ready and be around so they could help Dahlia feel more comfortable about her stay. When she finally got into the passenger seat, Willie jumping over her lap and then scrambling into the back, Grant weighed his words.

"We're going to let the police and Ursula know that someone was poking around the cabin, watching through the windows. And everyone

at Hudson Ranch will be on the lookout for anyone following you. We'll get to the bottom of it
in no time."

Grant started the truck and pushed it into
Drive.

"This sounds like a lot more than investigating a cold case."

"Cold cases sometimes warm up, Ms. Easton."
While he wanted to write it off as some kind of
Peeping Tom, the facts just didn't add up. "And
when they do, we protect whoever is in the cross
fire."

IT WAS PROBABLY supposed to be comforting, but
Dahlia couldn't relax sitting in the passenger seat
of Grant's truck. He kept those dark eyes trained
on the road and his mouth in a firm, tense line.

Dahlia glanced behind her at the dog, who sat
in the backseat panting happily.

If this was the *cross fire*, as Grant had so help-
fully put it, she supposed it wasn't all bad. And
she supposed if the cold case was warm, that
meant—had to mean—they were on to something with Truth.

He retraced the route she'd taken this morning. From her cabin to the sprawling Wyoming
ranch. She hadn't known real people lived like
this. The Hudsons had to be loaded. She didn't
know anything about ranching, but the sheer size
of their operation had to cost a bundle. And while

she knew she was paying for the Hudsons' services, she didn't think even that would fund all this. Even if they had a hundred cold cases they were solving for a fee.

Grant pulled the truck to a stop in front of the house.

"What about talking to the police?" she asked. Something about the house was so…inviting. Comforting. She had a hard time trusting it.

"Yeah, we'll take care of all of that at dinner." Grant got out of the truck, the dog bounding after him. Dahlia had no choice but to follow.

Grant was carrying her suitcase toward the house, and the dog ran off into the fields barking happily, and Dahlia could only scurry after Grant's long-legged strides.

"At dinner?"

"My oldest brother. He's Sunrise's sheriff. We'll tell him all about it at dinner. Just a forewarning though, whatever my brothers say about me and Truth, it isn't true."

She just stared at him. *Me and Truth.* Like he had some kind of deep dark secret about the place she was *sure* connected to her sister's disappearance.

He laughed, and that was something of a surprise in and of itself. Thus far, he'd been stern or overly polite. Not *amused*.

"I'm sorry," he said, and seemed genuinely

apologetic. "Not in some scary I-was-in-a-cult way. Truth's been a ghost town since we were born. I think you can imagine what teenage boys do in ghost towns, but if you can't, they spend a lot of time trying to scare the tar out of each other."

"Oh."

He opened the front door and gestured her in. She hesitated, because surely everything she was doing was silly. She could hear her father's voice in her head: *Everything too good to be true usually is.*

But Grant was inside with her things. He handed the suitcase off to Mary, who was apparently waiting for their arrival.

"I know the Meadowlark Cabin is so cute and a great place to relax," she said, reaching forward and taking Dahlia's arm. "But we've got a nice room for you, a private bathroom, and you'll be safe and sound until everyone can get to the bottom of everything."

And then Dahlia was being firmly maneuvered deeper into the gorgeous house. She glanced back at Grant, who was standing there still looking like that stern cowboy.

But he'd investigated. He'd warned her about someone watching her. And he'd laughed when telling her about teenage shenanigans.

Mary led her up a staircase. "This is sort of the

guest wing," she explained. "So, you'll have privacy for the most part in this hallway, and there's an en suite bath in your room."

Before Dahlia could protest once again, Mary kept right on. "I know it likely feels strange to come stay at a stranger's house. But I just want you to know this isn't out of the ordinary for us. We've put up clients before. Sometimes it's easier to accomplish things if people are on the premises."

But this wasn't about accomplishing things. It was, allegedly, about keeping her safe.

Mary opened a door and gestured Dahlia inside. The room was spacious and beautiful. The walls a buttery yellow with floral prints. There were lace curtains over the big windows. The bed had that Western quality of somehow looking both feminine and inviting and big and sturdy.

"If there's anything I can do to put you at ease, if you want to have someone join you—your parents, a friend? There's no extra charge for that. There's a lock on the door, a phone in the room. Bathroom is through there with any toiletry you might need, but if not, ask. Think of it as a bed-and-breakfast."

"I'm not paying you for a bed-and-breakfast."

Mary smiled kindly. "You're paying us for a service. This is part of the service if it needs to be. Unpack. Relax. I'll come get you for dinner."

There was nothing to say. Mary was already gone, leaving Dahlia alone in this…truly perfect room.

She stepped to the window and pulled the lace curtain back, looking out over the ranch. Everything about it was beautiful. The grassland, the mountains in the distance, the buildings and fences that dotted the landscape looking both old and impeccable at the same time.

Rose would love it because it was generations and roots and legacy. She would be throwing herself into these people, what they knew and how they all connected.

But Dahlia wasn't her sister. She couldn't get past how wrong this all felt. No matter how genuine Mary seemed or how capable Grant *was*. She didn't belong in their home.

Someone *had* been watching her though, she couldn't deny that or be okay with it. She'd felt it at times and brushed it off. It irritated her that Grant didn't believe the connections she'd found, even as she understood why he'd be skeptical, but he *had* protected her and listened to her even when he didn't believe her.

She supposed there was something noble in what the Hudsons were doing, trying to solve cold cases. She'd picked them for not just their proximity to Truth but because the story on their website had been about their own parents' cold case.

Dahlia wanted to believe they cared because of that connection even if her own cynicism held her back sometimes, but this seemed too good to be true.

And her father had always warned her about that.

She sighed and stepped away from the window. She didn't unpack. She just…sat down on the bed and tried to get a handle on her roiling emotions.

The next thing she knew, someone was knocking at the door. She'd fallen asleep, clearly, though she didn't remember lying down. Drowsily, she got back up and realized outside the sun was starting to set.

Mary was at the door with that kind smile on her face. "Hungry?" she asked.

Dahlia didn't have a chance to respond before Mary was leading her out of the room, back down the stairs, through the living room she'd initially met Grant in and then to a whole new wing of the house.

She heard voices—raucous but pleasant—before she entered the room. Mary led her into the spacious dining room dominated by a long table and *lots* of people. The chairs at the table were nearly all full. Grant and three carbon copies of him, a woman who was currently arguing loudly with one of them and then a girl not more than ten or eleven who was feeding scraps to the three dogs patiently waiting under the table.

The table itself had a huge family-style meal, bowls and platters overflowing with food. It looked like Christmas or some big family celebration, but Dahlia could tell by the way they acted, it was just the norm for them.

Mary gave her arm a little tug and then gestured her to a seat. "Dahlia, this is everyone," she said, as the voices around the table quieted. "We've got the brothers Jack, Cash, Palmer, and you know Grant. My sister Anna. Cash's daughter Izzy. Don't bother trying to remember all the dogs' names. Half of them look alike, and they're all running around constantly. Now, you sit right here and help yourself."

Dahlia was already overwhelmed, and she wasn't sure she'd caught any of those names. None of this felt…right. She cleared her throat and did not sit down. "I do appreciate this. I really do. But I shouldn't be interrupting your family dinner. I'm not paying for room and board. I'm—"

"We charge for work. That's honest," Jack said, with a firm nod. "We don't charge for hospitality—not when we've got plenty to spare. Now, sit and eat up. You need it."

Dahlia didn't know how to argue with that, particularly coming from a stony-faced man who looked even more like a cowboy out of an old Western than Grant did, complete with shiny star badge pinned to his shirt.

Dahlia slowly sank into the seat. Grant himself

put a heaping pile of mashed potatoes on her plate before passing them along to Mary next to her.

He gave her a reassuring nod. "I'd advise you listen. No one argues with Jack's hard head and wins."

So Dahlia did just that.

Chapter Five

Grant hadn't slept well. He'd gone over Dahlia Easton's case again and again, adding his own experiences, and felt no closer to a lead than he had when the Peeping Tom, or whoever was watching her, got away.

He wanted to prove that Eugene Green and Truth had nothing to do with her sister's disappearance, but no matter how little he *thought* they connected, he hadn't found a way to prove they didn't.

And that bothered him.

Still, he was up at dawn with his brothers to handle the necessary ranch chores. Some things they hired out, but the brothers always met in the mornings to handle a few jobs like all the Hudsons had since they'd arrived in Sunrise over a hundred years ago.

He met them at the stables, same as every morning since they'd been kids. But only Palmer and Cash were there.

"Where's Jack?"

"Went in early," Palmer said, pulling his hat lower on his head against the rising sun. He looked like he'd been out late last night, probably drinking, but Grant said nothing about that, as he was already in a terrible mood.

"Said he was going to take pictures of those footprints and write up a report. Have one of his deputies check around, see if anyone's seen anything suspicious," Cash added.

"That's good." Grant envied him. It was an actionable step to take. Take a report. Collect evidence. *Do* something instead of read the same reports over and over again.

"She's a looker," Palmer offered.

Grant could have pretended he didn't know who his brother was talking about, but he didn't see the point. "She's a client," Grant replied irritably. And sure, pretty as a spring day. But she was barking up all kinds of wrong trees.

Case in point: Eugene Green. "Cash, you looked at the file?"

Cash nodded in assent as they all got up on the horses. They didn't have to talk about what they were doing today. Jack kept a strict calendar and schedule, and he always made sure everyone knew what their role for the day was.

"What do you make of this attempt at a Eugene Green connection?"

"Well." Cash took his time responding as their horses walked side by side through the cool, pretty morning. "The security picture she's got is grainy at best, but you can't discount some similarities to Eugene Green."

"The guy was a lunatic. He could have had kids all over the country," Palmer added.

"Ones that wouldn't necessarily know a thing about him," Cash pointed out.

"It could also be a coincidence," Grant said. "Reaching."

"Could," Cash replied, and once again let silence settle over them. Because Cash was never in a hurry. He took his time to draw any conclusions. "But it's not the only connection to Eugene Green. The missing sister was all up in these DNA tests and whatever."

"Can't those things be wrong?" Palmer asked.

"Anything can be wrong. But it could just as easily be right." Cash looked over at Grant and shrugged. "I know you want to. I get why. But we can't discount the facts."

"I'll take over this one if you want." Palmer flashed a grin. "I'd take Red *very* seriously."

Grant didn't know why that comment set his teeth on edge. His brother was forever saying things like that and making his way through the female population of Sunrise and just about every surrounding area. And somehow, he hadn't ticked off the wrong woman yet.

"Take her over to Mrs. Riley this morning. She'd know all about the Green family tree and all that. More than any DNA ancestry site or just about anyone else. I know you don't *want* it to connect to Truth, but we all know how cold cases like this go. Any little connection can lead you to a bigger one."

It was a solid idea and an honest lecture. Grant didn't care for either from his little brother. "Maybe *you* should take over the case?"

Cash looked wistful for a fraction of a second before he was shaking his head and nudging his horse in the other direction. "Gotta get Izzy off to school. Then I'll be working with the dogs. Call if you need anything."

"Dumb thing to say," Palmer muttered once Cash was out of earshot.

"Well, he should take some cases. He can't *never* leave the ranch just because he's got a daughter."

"His choice," Palmer replied.

Because when push came to shove, the two younger brothers tended to stick together. And Grant didn't have Jack here to be on *his* side, though no doubt Jack would be.

So Grant worked with Palmer in mostly silence until breakfast time, then broke off and headed back to the house. Cash's suggestion was a good one. He'd take Dahlia over to the library today and maybe stop by the sheriff's department and check on things.

It wasn't going to connect to Eugene Green.

It probably wasn't going to connect to anything. But for all of Dahlia Easton's more...fragile tendencies, she was determined to see this through. Stubborn, no doubt.

So, if nothing else, he had to *disprove* a theory that was going to lead her on a wild-goose chase. And maybe Cash was right and they could find some bigger more plausible thread to tug.

He couldn't help but think of the way she'd clearly been so lost and overwhelmed at dinner last night. He couldn't blame her—the Hudson clan could be overwhelming even when you were one of them—but he knew in part it was hard for her, because they were a family, and she was missing a piece of hers.

But so were they. And had been since their parents had gone missing all those years ago. He should have said something about it, should have made the connection to her so she might have felt some...sliver of comfort.

But he'd just filled up her plate and watched to make sure she ate and then let Mary handle things from there.

He was the investigator, and his job was to find answers. Even knowing there might never be any answers to give.

He got to the stables and took care of his horse before walking back to the house. He saw a figure sitting on the side porch and realized that flash of red meant it wasn't his family or a ranch hand but the woman in question.

He walked toward her, though there was an odd, errant bolt of a thought that told him he should turn around. Go anywhere but forward. But that made absolutely no sense, so he walked forward. To the porch, to Dahlia.

She sat on the little rocking chair his grandmother had liked to do her knitting on in the summer. In the here and now, Dahlia had a mug of coffee cupped between her hands. Her red hair whipped around in the breeze, and she watched him approach with careful eyes.

She looked exactly right there, like she'd been born to sit on his porch and wait for him to arrive. Which was the strangest damn thought he'd ever had, perhaps, in his entire life and left him completely mute.

She didn't say anything either. For a lot longer than made sense. Eventually she broke the silence.

"I expected a *howdy* maybe."

His mouth quirked. "Fresh out." His voice sounded gruffer than it should have, so he cleared his throat. "The library in town has all sorts of things on Truth, as does the genealogy society, which has an office in the library. Why don't we eat breakfast and head over? We'll stop by the sheriff's department, see if they've found anything about the guy watching you."

She didn't say anything to that, just kept watching him with those careful eyes. Wary.

He didn't have any right to be frustrated, but it bothered him all the same. For reasons he couldn't begin to sort out. "It must be hard to trust perfect strangers, even if you are paying them. Doesn't hurt my feelings. But I do know things would be easier if you'd give us a chance."

"I'm here, aren't I?"

"You are. And just about always looking for the rattlesnake to strike." He could understand it and still be frustrated by it. Apparently that was going to be his predominant feeling around Dahlia.

But the breeze teased the red waves of her hair, and her blue eyes held his in an eerie silence that settled over him like a touch.

Okay, maybe not the *predominant feeling.*

Then she blinked and gave a little nod. "You're not the enemy is what you're getting at, and treating you like one probably doesn't move the needle any closer to finding answers."

"That's a good way of putting it."

"I've been looking for help for a year. Someone, anyone to take me or Rose seriously. Even my parents don't."

He thought she might break at the mention of her parents. She looked on the cusp of tears and Grant wanted to back away from *that.* She straightened her shoulders though. Blinked back the tears.

"I've been fighting *everyone* for answers. Even the people who've helped... It only lasts for so long. At a certain point, you can only depend on yourself."

He hadn't expected her words to cut him off at the knees, but they did. Because he knew that feeling. Was so well acquainted with it, it had helped build HSS—the fact that, eventually, he and his siblings hadn't had anyone else to lean on. They'd learned that when faced with something difficult, they could only trust themselves.

But he had his siblings. He had family and roots, and Dahlia Easton didn't seem to have much of anything.

"At a certain point, I hope you feel like you can depend on us, but even if you never feel that way, we'll see this through. That's a promise."

She looked down at her coffee. He wasn't sure it was disagreement or just feeling overwhelmed, but she didn't lift her gaze again when she spoke. "When do we go to this library?"

DAHLIA HADN'T WANTED to eat breakfast. She'd slept better last night than she had since she'd left Minnesota, but her stomach still roiled and made it hard to feel like eating—even if last night's dinner had been delicious.

Still, much like last night, somehow Grant maneuvered her into eating a small plate of eggs and toast. And, though she didn't plan on admitting out loud to anyone, it did make her feel sturdier. More like she was capable of surviving this strange new world she found herself in.

Maybe—she could admit in the privacy of her own head—she hadn't been taking care of herself very well. Maybe she needed to if she was going to actually get to the bottom of Rose's disappearance.

Then she'd had to go out with Grant and climb into his big intimidating truck, this time without her dog friend as company. She did have Rose's binder replicas though, and she clutched them too hard as Grant drove them into town.

"Do you think your library will have something my sister didn't?"

"It's possible. Not everything's on the internet, especially when it comes to a small town like Sunrise, and it seems as though Rose didn't make a connection to Wyoming until she got to Texas, right?"

"As far as I know."

"So, she didn't make it here. Which means there might be records or clues into the family connection that might lead us to an answer."

He didn't believe it was Truth or Eugene Green. She kept telling herself it didn't matter. People believing her hadn't mattered this whole time, so why should it start now?

But she found herself wanting to explain to him until he agreed with her. Luckily, she'd learned when to keep her mouth shut, even when she didn't want to. Maybe her parents had taught her something worthwhile after all.

He didn't try to fill the silence as he drove—off the sprawling Hudson Ranch and toward the town of Sunrise.

It was beautiful. The whole area—ranch or driving or even the cute little western town. Dahlia had always planned on visiting the West at some point. Make it out to Yellowstone or even Colorado, but school and then work had taken up most of her time, and when she finally went on vacations, it was always with Rose, who preferred cities or old museums on the East Coast.

But there was something so open and vast about Wyoming. Sunrise was just a postage stamp of a town that clustered around the main thoroughfare. And in the distance, craggy peaks that felt intimidating or awe-inspiring depending on the moment.

Grant pulled his truck into a parking spot in front of a squat stone building that didn't look like much, except old. But as they got up and walked to the door, Dahlia noted the little details that made it special. Impressive little cornices shaped like books. Tiny books carved into the wood frame around the door. She followed Grant inside. Small, definitely, but…warm. Inviting. So much more so than the new, more industrial-like building her library was housed in back home.

The woman behind the desk looked up, then straightened a little as if she recognized Grant. When she flashed him a smile, Dahlia was *sure* she recognized him.

"Hi there, Freya," he offered somewhat absently, like he didn't notice the woman brighten the minute she laid eyes on him.

"Morning, Grant." Her eyes flicked to Dahlia, and the smile dimmed a little. But she held firm. "Here for work?"

Grant nodded, then gestured at Dahlia. "This is Ms. Easton."

"Hi," Freya offered, and though she was definitely speculating about some things based on the way she gave Dahlia a once-over, Dahlia didn't feel any animosity. Exactly.

"Is Mrs. Riley in?"

"Just like always," Freya said, trying to share a conspiratorial eye roll with Grant, but Dahlia watched him miss it, as he was already looking deeper into the library, presumably for Mrs. Riley.

"Thanks," he said, not giving poor Freya a second look. Dahlia moved to follow Grant, but something about Freya's crestfallen expression made her stop.

"I love what you've done with this place. It's so inviting. I'm a librarian in Minnesota, and everything is so…bureaucratic. I can't make any choices about decor without like three people writing off on it."

"Oh well. Probably a little bigger than this, huh?" Freya sounded wistful again.

"But not nearly as special."

The corner of Freya's mouth tugged up, and she looked around as if seeing the library with new eyes. "Thanks. It really is cozy, isn't it?"

"I love it." She smiled and then followed Grant, who was waiting by a door with a somewhat impatient frown on his face.

Once she approached, he knocked on the door.

Dahlia felt like she should probably keep her mouth shut, but Grant seemed totally ignorant. "She likes you."

He frowned at her, then over at Freya. "She dated my brother."

Well, that did change things, Dahlia supposed. She glanced back at Freya. "Well, regardless of what she *did*, she's currently very into *you*."

Grant grunted and said nothing more as the door opened to an older woman. She looked at Grant, then Dahlia.

"Your turn, huh?" the woman said to Grant.

He nodded. "Mrs. Riley, this is Dahlia Easton. Ms. Easton, this is Mrs. Riley. She runs the historical society, the genealogical society and knows just about everything about the history of Sunrise."

Mrs. Riley eyed Dahlia with some suspicion.

Dahlia wondered if this was the small-town distrust of outsiders she'd read about but never experienced.

"Come on in then." She waved them into the cramped room. Shelves lined two walls filled with labeled binders and boxes. She had a little table in the middle of the room—also filled with stacks of folders, books and binders. Then the two chairs in the room were filled with stacks as well.

"So, what are you wanting to know?"

"I'd like to ask for your discretion before we show you anything," Grant said.

Mrs. Riley grinned, a flash of a woman with *some* sense of humor. "You can ask."

Grant sighed but didn't argue with her. "Ms. Easton's sister was tracing her family tree when she disappeared over a year ago. Ms. Easton found some…loose connections to Sunrise and—"

"Not to Sunrise," Dahlia interrupted. "To Truth. To the Greens."

Grant closed his eyes as if in pain. Mrs. Riley's bland expression went into a furious scowl, but Dahlia paid no heed. She took her binder, opened it to the page that had led her here and handed it to Mrs. Riley.

The woman looked at the page, then back at Dahlia, eyes narrowed as she pointed to the section on the Greens. "How'd you find out about this?"

"Wait. *You* know about this Texas connection?" Grant asked Mrs. Riley.

"Of course I do," the woman replied with a sniff. "I made sure I knew every last inch of that family so they could never hurt mine again." Then her gaze turned to Dahlia, and it was *cold*. "Guess you're one of them."

"It's a loose connection at best," Dahlia replied, but that didn't win her any favors.

"*Loose* wouldn't matter to the Greens." Mrs. Riley tapped her bright pink fingernails on the book. "The cult was big into blood ties and rituals. He'd have known his tree backward and forward. He'd have known about *you*. Which is why I asked, how'd you know about this?"

"I didn't. My sister did research and took a DNA test." *And disappeared.*

"Eugene Green is dead, Mrs. Riley. We all know that," Grant said, as if he said it firmly enough, this woman would simply have to accept it.

Mrs. Riley huffed. "Maybe. Maybe not. There're rumors, and some of them connect to Texas."

Grant muttered something that sounded like "God save me from conspiracy theories," but Mrs. Riley didn't seem to catch it.

She turned away from the binder Dahlia held out. "I don't need any Greens hanging around *my* office."

"You're not—" But Grant didn't finish the sentence. Mrs. Riley folded her arms across her chest and just glared.

It wasn't exactly a dead end, Dahlia assured herself as she followed Grant out of the small office. If Mrs. Riley knew about conspiracy theories that connected to an alive Eugene Green in Texas, there was a chance someone else in town knew about it.

She waved at Freya as they passed, and Grant gave the woman an absent nod at best before they stepped back into the pretty fall morning.

"I'm sorry about that. I did *not* see that coming, but I should have."

"It's not a big deal."

"It is to me. It isn't right to hold people accountable for some random offshoot of a family you didn't even know about." He sounded strangely vehement. Like he'd…maybe dealt with similar before.

"It isn't right my sister is gone," Dahlia said gently. "The world doesn't work on what's right."

He grunted, clearly not loving that answer. What must it be like to be a man who went through life thinking he could make everything right simply through sheer force of will?

"The sheriff's department is just down the street. How about a walk?"

Dahlia thought he made the suggestion for himself. He was a contained man, but frustrated energy pumped off him. So she agreed and fell into step beside him as they walked down the sidewalk.

She still clutched the binder to her chest. She looked down at it, then at the frustrated man next to her.

"It isn't about me. Mrs. Riley being upset. It's about her...life. I don't know what the Greens did to her, I don't need to know in order to understand."

"That's very generous of you," Grant replied. He looked down at her, and something in his expression softened. "You want it to be a lead, but they're just stories. And Mrs. Riley is going to tell *everyone*, so it's going to be all stories and conspiracy theories. I think there's one about aliens? It's going to get ridiculous, and I just want you to understand these aren't leads. If there was any truth to all the stories that fly around about Truth and the Greens, the authorities would have found that out a long time ago. It's not hope. Trust me, I have been there, and all it does is prolong the pain."

She wanted to bristle, but she heard a world of experience in his words. He had been there, she knew, because they had the story of their parents' disappearance on their website. They promised dedication and hard work because they knew what not having answers felt like.

Still felt like.

"How does it not eat you alive?" she asked, her voice a mere whisper. She knew she shouldn't ask. It wasn't polite, and what's more, she was almost certain she'd hate the answer.

"It's always eating you alive," Grant replied softly. "You just have to do other things while it does."

Which was *dire* and not at all hopeful. "Forever?"

"If it's forever." He glanced at her. All dark-eyed intensity. But also…a pain under it all. She supposed it drove him—all of them. She'd only been missing her sister a year. They'd been missing their parents for over a decade.

"So, you still have hope for your parents?" she asked, *had* to. Because it seemed hope was the source of the pain, but Dahlia knew it was also the source of everything that kept *her* going. Did that die at some point? Would she be left with… nothing?

"I wish I didn't," he said, looking away, jaw clenched. Unknown years of pain in every syllable of those words.

"That's not a no."

He stopped in front of a door and hesitated, which didn't seem to fit the man at all. But in the end, he didn't respond to her. He gestured at the door that read *Sunrise Sheriff's Department*.

"Come on. Let's go talk to my brother."

Chapter Six

Jack had found the footprints at the rental cabin, and he had a deputy working on questioning anyone who might have been around the Meadowlark Cabin while Dahlia had been there. There were no clear answers on who might be watching her. Unfortunately, it wasn't looking good they'd find any, unless they caught the watcher in the act in the future.

Grant didn't like it. The idea she might be in danger and the idea the woman who was stirring up Truth talk would be under his roof for the foreseeable future.

But she'd answered Jack's questions carefully and concisely. She'd asked a few of her own about what she should be doing to keep herself safe.

She seemed to be in better shape than she had yesterday, and he didn't know why that gave him some odd sense of satisfaction. Like he'd had anything to do with it, even if he *had* all but tricked her into eating breakfast this morning.

After Jack was satisfied, Grant drove Dahlia

back to the ranch in silence. He'd give her credit, she didn't seem to mind the silence. It settled over them easily enough. He supposed they were both lost in their own thoughts, worries. Hopes.

He scowled at the road in front of him. He didn't allow himself to think much on *hope*. He focused on reality. Facts. Probability.

In all *likelihood*, his parents were long dead. If they weren't, it still wasn't a *good* story. But no matter how his brain told him those things, over and over again since he'd been a teenager, his heart still wanted a different outcome.

Which was damn foolish.

He pulled the truck in front of the house. He wasn't sure what to do with Dahlia. Usually when he investigated a case, the person looking for answers wasn't his responsibility to cart around.

Maybe he'd dump her on Mary while he tried to figure out what the next step would be to get ahead of all the Truth gossip.

When Dahlia got out of the car, Grant heard the yip of a dog. Willie came racing around the corner and zoomed straight for Dahlia. Jumping and yapping happily as if they were long-lost loves.

Dahlia knelt and accepted the dog's excited kisses while she rubbed him down. "There's my hero."

Something uncomfortable and unacceptable tangled low in his gut as she smiled at the dog. For a second, her worries had lifted, and he wished with an intensity the situation didn't warrant he could give her that kind of happiness long term.

But some cold cases were never solved, as he well knew.

That's not a no.

He *knew* his parents were dead. Knew it.

Palmer appeared on the porch. "Good. You're home. I've got something to show you." He glanced at Dahlia. "You and Willie can come too, Ms. Easton."

Her smile faded as she stood. "I suppose that means it's about me."

Palmer shrugged apologetically, then waved them to follow. Not through the house but around it, back where Willie had run from. Grant walked toward the fence that wrapped around the front and back yards—more for decoration and land demarcation rather than keeping the animals in one place or the usual functional ranch fences.

As they walked, Willie kept right next to Dahlia. She seemed to relax around the dog, so Grant made a mental note to see if Cash would let Willie stick around the main house until they figured out if Dahlia was safe.

"Are you the brother the librarian dated?" Dahlia asked as they walked.

Palmer looked back at Grant with raised eyebrows. "Freya? Yeah, we went out a few times a few years ago."

Dahlia frowned at him, as if she objected to his term *date* when explained in that way. But she didn't know Palmer. A few dates *was* about as close to a relationship as he ever got.

"So, it was nothing serious for Grant to worry about," Dahlia continued.

"Grant?" Palmer laughed. "She's always had a thing for Grant. Long before she went out with me, but he doesn't date local women." Palmer grinned at him over Dahlia's head. "Or much at all. Everyone knows that. Including Freya."

"I'm glad we can discuss everyone's private life so openly, but I'd prefer to focus on the case." Grant didn't shove his hands into his pockets like he wanted or hunch his shoulders. He remained passive. Blank.

Palmer jerked a thumb in Grant's direction but leaned down to stage-whisper conspiratorially to Dahlia. "All work, no play, this one."

Grant didn't like the serious bolt of anger and frustration that shot through him when Palmer was just being Palmer. Trying to get a rise out of him. It wasn't anything Grant hadn't heard before.

Dahlia smiled a little at Palmer's quip, but she didn't quite jump in as Palmer likely hoped or Grant expected.

"I suppose it's important work," she said instead.

Palmer rolled his eyes but stopped at the

fence line around the front yard. "Found some footprints. Not any of ours and shouldn't be a ranch hand's." He glanced at Dahlia and tried to smile reassuringly. "Doesn't mean they're not, of course."

Grant wanted to swear, but he held it in. All the tension that had gone out of her shoulders at Willie's arrival was back.

"I don't really understand this," she said, looking at the clear set of footprints in the mud.

"Did you call Jack?" Grant asked.

Palmer nodded. "Took some pictures and sent them over. Deputies are all tied up, but they'll be by eventually. Haven't told Cash yet. He's going to flip."

"Why?" Dahlia asked, directing the question at him rather than Palmer.

"Cash…worries," Grant said, trying for diplomacy. "Izzy likes to wander."

"The daughter," Dahlia said, chewing on her bottom lip. "Should I not stay here? I don't want to bring trouble to your door. That isn't—"

"We can handle it," Grant assured her. "You've got the sheriff living on the premises, along with trained investigative professionals. We have a great security system, which Palmer can assure you is some of the best."

"I make sure of it. Plus, this guy here is a war hero."

Dahlia's eyes widened as she turned to him again. "War hero?"

Grant tried not to react to the term. He hated it. He hadn't done anything special—except survive when a lot of men hadn't. "I was a Marine. Doesn't make me a war hero."

"That's not what the paper said when he came home."

"Can we focus on the task at hand?" Grant said, failing at keeping the snap out of his tone. "Dahlia, I'd like you to go inside. I'm going to look around and see what else I can find."

She frowned at that, then looked down at Willie sitting next to her. "I'd like to look too. I feel like…" She struggled over whatever she wanted her next words to be. "I just want to know what I should keep an eye out for. Does that make sense?"

Grant exchanged a look with Palmer. He didn't really want Dahlia tagging along, but it was hard to refuse someone who wanted to learn in order to protect themselves.

"I'll go break the news to Cash before he hears it through the grapevine. Text if you find anything else. Jack will call Mary when they've got a deputy on the way, but it won't hurt to have it checked out before they get there."

"All right. Tell Cash we're keeping Willie with us for the time being."

"Will do." With that, Palmer left, and Grant

had to decide how best to handle a woman and a dog when he'd much prefer to search alone.

"Grant, I really don't understand why someone would be watching me."

"Neither do I, which is why we're going to get to the bottom of it. We're going to see how far we can follow these footprints." He looked the way the footprints were pointing. There was no clear glimpse *into* the house from here, but that didn't mean they hadn't searched for other places. "Now, make sure you follow me. We don't want a bunch of extra prints. We want the police to know exactly what they're looking at."

Dahlia nodded solemnly. "What about Willie?"

"Willie knows how to follow orders."

"Oh."

Grant studied the footprints, then hopped the fence a good few feet away so he wouldn't disturb them. Willie wriggled under the bottom rung, but Dahlia stood there looking unsure.

She was dressed in jeans and tennis shoes and a winter coat, and the fence was low and easy to climb over, so he wasn't sure what held her back. "Do you need help?"

"No." But she looked so unsure as she awkwardly maneuvered over the fence. Grant took a step toward her as if to steady her. But she got on the other side without tripping or toppling over.

She offered him a rueful smile. "I'm not very athletic." She steadied herself on the fence instead of his outstretched hand. "I can follow directions though."

He thought about yesterday when she'd gone off to Truth by herself. He supposed he hadn't directed her *not* to, but it didn't exactly speak to compliance.

Still, he gestured her forward, because she definitely deserved to know what to be on the lookout for when she was the target.

DAHLIA FOLLOWED GRANT, though her tennis shoes weren't holding up very well against the mud they tramped through. But it was a fairly good landscape to see footprints in.

Or so said Grant. He pointed to little marks, indentations and holes and actual outlines she could see. There were paw prints and other signs of animal activity. He explained each of them to her patiently and as if it were important information to know.

She supposed for him it was. So she listened and filed away what she could. But she'd never been an outdoorsy person. She preferred books and being able to control the temperature of the room she was in.

They walked and walked, and every once in a while, Grant would stop, crouch, study another print. When they were human, or he thought they were, he pulled out his phone and took a picture.

Willie followed along, right beside her, never darting off, though sometimes he would stop, sniff and let out a faint *woof.*

Dahlia had always wanted a dog, but her father and Rose had been allergic, and then when she'd finally moved out at Rose's insistence, her apartment hadn't allowed pets. She should think about getting one in the future, but she couldn't seem to see a future anymore.

There was just finding Rose or finding out what had happened to her. Everything else was... not important.

So she walked with Grant. In silence. Dahlia didn't usually mind that, but the conversation with Palmer had given little glimpses into Grant the man. Which she supposed was none of her business, but she was staying under their roof for the time being. They were helping her.

Why not know more?

"So, Jack is law enforcement, Cash handles the dogs, and Palmer is the security. Mary does all the administrative work, but what do you and your other sister specialize in?"

"Anna is a private investigator. She likes the flexibility of going off and working for herself when she needs to."

He did not answer in regard to himself. When she slid in a little mud, he immediately reached out and grabbed her arm, helping her stay upright. Once she was, he immediately dropped it and kept on walking.

"And you?" she pressed. It wasn't usual for her to press, but something about this man's tight-lipped nature made her want to.

He shrugged, knelt and studied another print. "I fill in where needed."

"Jack of all trades?"

"Guess so. They all started this when I was still deployed, and they weren't sure when I'd be coming home. This is animal," he said, standing again and then moving forward.

There was something about the way he said *deployed*, devoid of just enough emotion to make her curious. He didn't sound bitter or resentful, but there was a tenseness to him when he or Palmer spoke of his military career.

She thought military made perfect sense. He was so…large. So self-possessed. It wasn't hard at all to imagine him in military camo holding one of those big intimidating weapons. If that was what Marines did. She didn't know.

But Palmer had called him a war hero.

"Where were you dep—"

"Look, it's not interesting. The military is the military. I didn't do anything special. I'm not a hero. I joined the Marines at eighteen. I did my time, went on a few deployments, did as I was told, watched out for my brothers and when my final time was up, I came home. Beginning and end of story."

Dahlia didn't argue with him, though she inexplicably wanted to. She couldn't imagine being any kind of soldier, away from home, in this weird system of guns and violence and war. So it *was* kind of interesting…intriguing. Courageous.

But she could also imagine why he might not want to talk about it. So she bit her tongue and kept following Grant, Willie happily trotting beside her.

The next time Grant crouched at a print, even Dahlia could see it was a footprint. They were more toward the back of the house now. If she put her feet where the prints were, she'd be looking at the back window.

She studied the house, trying not to let the fear take over like it had yesterday. But that was the window to the room she was staying in. Not that whoever stood here would be able to see in, but after yesterday, everything about this felt ominous and terrible.

"Both of these full prints are very similar to the one outside the cabin yesterday," Grant said, taking pictures from different angles. "Which leads me to believe it's the same person."

Dahlia nodded. Same person. Someone was… stalking her, basically. And as she wasn't interesting and hadn't made any enemies in her life, there seemed to be only one logical conclusion.

"If someone…" She struggled with the next word, emotionally and being able to say it past all that emotion. "If someone murdered Rose, they wouldn't want people poking around her disappearance, would they?"

She thought she might surprise him with the question, but he only looked grim. Like it had already crossed his mind. Like he already believed it.

A shudder of worry went through her. Her parents had warned her she was getting in over her head. Were they right?

"It's only one theory," Grant said gently, but she knew just by the fact he was *being* gentle, it was the most logical one.

"Even if it's true, even if she's dead, I can't give up. I have to find out what happened."

"Even if it puts you in danger?"

Dahlia looked from the footprint to the mountains in the distance. Such a pretty place, and someone out there was watching her. But they hadn't done anything to hurt her.

The *yet* seemed to hang in the air around her.

"I can't live with myself if I go back home. If I put it all away. I just can't." She met Grant's direct brown gaze. Maybe he didn't understand or couldn't, but maybe she didn't need anyone to understand except herself. "I'd rather risk something than try to live under the weight of not doing anything."

For a moment they stood there staring at each other in a grave silence. Then, finally, he nodded. "Let's go inside and update Jack and talk to Palmer about increasing some security measures."

Chapter Seven

Grant made sure Dahlia got back to her room, Willie in tow, then had his usual afternoon meeting with his siblings.

They discussed increased security, which wasn't the first time. Cold cases were often just that, cold, and came with no immediate danger, but they'd found themselves in a few questionable situations before, which had led Mary to develop a coding system, just like security threat levels.

Today, they moved the ranch's security level from green to yellow.

Of course, this meant that Cash was missing from the HSS meeting, as he likely wouldn't let Izzy out of their remote cabin for the foreseeable future. Mary and Anna thought it was a travesty, but Grant figured none of the rest of them were parents, so they didn't really get a say in how Cash decided to keep his child safe.

"It has to be an out-of-towner," Jack said, clearly frustrated neither he nor his deputies had come up with any leads yet. "Maybe someone followed her."

Grant had gone through the same reasonings. Tried to convince himself this had nothing to do with Sunrise or, worse, Truth.

But there was absolutely no evidence to the contrary.

"Someone had been at Truth. Before she got here. That shell casing I found wasn't old, but it wasn't brand new."

"Kids," Jack scoffed.

"I want to believe that too."

"Look, if *Grant* is willing to consider the possibility of Truth being involved, I'd say that's some damning evidence right there," Anna put in.

"I'm not saying Truth is actually involved." Though Grant realized with every passing step in this investigation, he had a harder time dismissing it out of hand. "I'm saying someone has been hanging out in Truth lately. I'm saying Dahlia's being followed only after making the connection to her family history and Truth."

Grant looked at his older brother, whose expression gave nothing away.

Jack had taken care of them since the moment their parents had disappeared. He'd kept the ranch going, made sure they did their homework and were fed and became responsible adults. Even though Grant had been sixteen himself, in a lot of ways, Jack had stepped into the role of fa-

ther despite the small two-year age difference
between them.

Grant had done everything he could to earn
Jack's approval, and it was hard now not to wither
under his older brother's stare. But these were
facts.

"My deputies will keep asking questions," Jack
said. "If she feels comfortable, I think it's best if
she stays here until we get to the bottom of it."

"I agree," Grant said with a nod. "I think she
will too, depending on how long it takes. But
she's pretty determined to get to the bottom of
what happened to her sister, even if it's bad news."

For a moment they were all silent because they
knew that even when you were determined, even
when you never gave up, sometimes answers
never materialized.

"I could post a deputy out here tonight. Be on
the lookout for someone."

"If Palmer and Anna are good with it, I think
we should just take turns in house. We'll have a
better sense of who should be coming and going
anyway."

"It's a big ranch."

"It is. But we all know nothing is getting by
Cash as long as Izzy is there. We've got the cameras at the entry points. We stay up and watch
them, maybe we can catch this guy."

"He's not setting the cameras off with movement," Palmer said. "I can change from mo-

tion-induced to twenty-four seven surveillance, but we'll have to up the security budget for the month."

"All in favor?" Jack asked, because he ran the business like a democracy even when he'd rather be dictator.

But wouldn't they all?

Everyone raised their hands, and Mary noted down the agreement so she could handle the funds. They tackled some other admin details, but Dahlia was their sole client right now, and with an active threat against her, it was hard to think about much else.

They ended the meeting and parted ways to go handle their individual jobs or chores. Grant *wanted* to throw himself into ranch work, but instead he settled in the big armchair in the office and went through Dahlia's binder all over again.

Eugene Green. Grant didn't for a second believe conspiracy theories. The man was dead, and the picture Dahlia had that *resembled* Eugene Green was grainy and fuzzy at best.

But she didn't think it *was* Eugene Green. She had said it could be someone that *looked* like him.

Grant flipped to the family tree again. Dahlia's family was an offshoot of what appeared to be a very normal branch that hadn't ever settled in Wyoming but had gone down to Texas. Before Dahlia had been born, her father had gone to college in the Midwest and married a native

Minnesotan, which is how she and her sister had ended up there.

He looked at the picture again. The woman identified as Rose Easton was just as grainy as the man, and the picture was black and white. There was a resemblance, he supposed, somewhere around the mouth and nose, between the woman and Dahlia. The resemblance between this man and Eugene Green as a young man easier to see.

But nothing about it was concrete, and Grant preferred to deal in concretes.

How was he going to find one?

He had to put it aside for dinner. One of the strictest family rules was everyone made it to dinner unless they had a *really* good excuse. Dahlia was already there when he entered the dining room. She still looked uncomfortable, but Willie was curled up behind her chair, and she was listening to Anna talk animatedly at her.

He took the seat next to her, and she offered a small smile as Anna continued to chatter and Mary brought out the food. It was the same kind of dinner as last night, except Cash, Izzy and a lot of the other dogs were missing. Dahlia was still quiet, but who could blame her with Anna and Palmer dominating the conversation like they usually did.

When they were done with dinner, he felt like he should say something to her about the fact that following the Eugene Green theory might lead them in the opposite direction, about the plans to keep her safe, so she could sleep tonight.

But in the end, she seemed content to talk to Mary and pet Willie, so Grant escaped the dining room with Palmer and went to their little security center—a small room on the first floor that had once been a porch before the house had been added on to in the fifties. It housed any of Palmer's security equipment, the guns they kept registered in their name locked in their respective safes and a computer.

Palmer booted it up. "I've changed all the cameras to run twenty-four seven like we discussed. It'll record everything, and I've armed the system on the house, but if we're worried the peeper might turn dangerous, we should keep physical watch."

Grant nodded in agreement. "Until we figure it out. Mary's always around, and I'll stick close to Dahlia."

"Yeah, I just bet you will."

Grant didn't rise to the bait. It wasn't worth it. "If her sister was murdered, this could be more dangerous than we originally thought."

"Always that possibility in a cold case. We're ready for it. I'll take the first shift," Palmer said. "Anna's second. You're the early bird, so you get third."

"All right. But come get me if anything is funny."

"Feeling territorial?"

Grant sighed. "How long are you going to try to get a rise out of me using that tactic?"

"Long as I think it might be true. I mean, she was interested in Freya's interest in you."

"I'm pretty sure that was to clear the way with Freya like some sort of ill-fated matchmaker."

"Nothing wrong with Freya."

"Nothing wrong with minding your own business either."

"Go get some shut-eye, bud."

Grant knew it was in his best interest to do just that. If Palmer took a four-hour shift, then Anna took a four, it would put him waking up at 4:00 a.m. Not much earlier than he usually got up, but he'd do better tomorrow if he got a good night's sleep and didn't stay up looking over every detail of the case he already knew by heart.

So, though he *wanted* to, he left his materials where they were in Mary's office, went to his room, got ready for bed and turned off every facet of his mind that wanted to think about Dahlia Easton and her case.

A trick he'd learned in the military that served him well. Still, sometime later, he awoke with a start, the taste of sand and blood in his mouth. An old dream he hadn't had in a long while making his heart pound like he'd just run a marathon.

He sat up in bed in the pitch-black and focused on getting his breathing back to even.

It was a mix of things—no one terrible memory from his service. A blend of them. A firefight here, a sniper there, sometimes his Marine brothers, sometimes his family members.

And this time a certain redhead who he certainly didn't want in his dreams, let alone as pale and bloody and very clearly dead as she had been.

It was hard—harder than it should have been—to get his breath back, so he slapped on his bedside light and did what he'd had to do almost every night when he'd first come home.

Focus on the little watermark on the ceiling. Count. Disassociate. Until his heart beat the way it should. Until his lungs moved easily—inhale, exhale—no hitch, no gulping for breath.

Just home and the reality that his days of war were behind him. He glanced at his clock: 3:15 a.m. Well, there was no point going back to bed for forty-five minutes when it'd likely take him that long to fall asleep after the nightmare.

So he got up, got dressed and went to find Anna in the security room. She was in the rolling chair, feet propped up on the table. She sipped a Coke while she watched the screens and clearly had earbuds in, so she didn't hear his approach.

Still, when he tapped on her shoulder, she didn't jump or startle at all. She just looked up at him, then swiveled around to face him as she pulled one of the buds out of her ear.

She frowned at him. "You're early—and looking a little ghostly," Anna said, studying him with way too perceptive hazel eyes. She looked almost exactly like their mother and acted *nothing* like her. She was the baby of the family, so Grant couldn't say how purposeful that was. She'd only been eight when Mom and Dad had disappeared, and sometimes Grant wondered how much of either of them she fully remembered.

"I'm fine," Grant muttered. He'd gotten a handle on the physical effects of the dream, but the emotional ones lingered.

"Haven't looked that way since—"

"I said I'm *fine*." He looked at the monitors Anna had been studying. "Nothing, huh?"

She paused as if deciding whether or not to argue, then swiveled back to look at the screens. "Not a thing. If he knows we're looking…"

"I think he'd have to be local to know we're looking."

"You were the one who told Jack he *could* be local. Besides, *he* could also be a *she*. You don't know."

Grant resisted rolling his eyes at his sister. Sure, it was possible, but it was a big boot print to be looking for a woman. He almost pointed that out, but something…moved. Grant's eyes narrowed. "Did you see that?"

"A shadow," Anna confirmed, leaning forward.

"That's way too close to where I saw a footprint this afternoon. The one that looked into Dahlia's room." He didn't like it, so he was already reaching for his gun.

"You can't go out there alone."

"Can. Will. Wake up Palmer. And get Dahlia out of that room."

"Don't you think—"

It would take too long. It would all take too long. "Get her out of that room," he repeated, then ran for the back door.

Chapter Eight

Dahlia was roused from sleep by a pounding on her door and the sound of a dog whining. Once she finally woke up enough to understand the noise—and how it couldn't mean anything good—she threw back the covers and rushed to the door.

She wasn't sure why she expected it to be Grant or why something in her chest sank when it was Anna instead.

"Hey, sorry to wake you," Anna said, reaching down to pet Willie. She was calm and even smiled, so maybe this wasn't…terrible.

"I… It's fine. What time is it?" But Anna had taken her arm and was pulling her forward and out of the room, Willie padding after them. Which didn't seem good at all when it was still dark everywhere.

"We might have caught our friend, but if he knows you're in this room, we just want to go above and beyond careful and get you into an interior room. If you're the target."

Target?

Why was she a target for anything?

But she knew there was only one answer to that, and it meant Rose was dead. So she pushed the thought away. Had to.

Anna pulled her down the hall, and Dahlia felt like she had no choice but to go. It was only when she was halfway down the corridor that she realized she was in her pajamas. Shorts and a baggy tee, fine enough, but not wearing a *bra* underneath. The floors were cold on her bare feet, and everything made her shiver.

Anna, on the other hand, was dressed like it was the middle of the day. Jeans, sweater, cowboy boots.

"Um." Dahlia hugged herself as the chill sank deeper.

Anna looked back. "Oh man, you're cold. I'll get you a sweatshirt or something. Let's just get you into our wing first."

Our wing?

It was a big house. Sprawling, really, and maybe like the wings had been added on over the years as the family expanded.

They crossed through the living room, where a big window overlooked the front yard. It was still only dark out there, but Dahlia saw the flash of red and blue lights.

"The police are here."

"Yeah. Hopefully they're arresting the jerk."

Anna looked back at her and then offered another smile. "Don't worry. It's all probably harmless. We're just being super cautious with the active part of this case."

Active? As though Rose missing *wasn't* active. Which made Dahlia's stomach twist into more knots.

They went through the dining room and then up a new set of stairs and down another hallway. Mary stepped out of a door in this hallway, also dressed as if it were the middle of the day, though her outfit was a little bit more *business* than Anna's ranch wear. Slacks, a button-down shirt and a cardigan.

Dahlia felt more and more out of place.

"Oh, I'm sure you're freezing," Mary said immediately. "I'll grab you a robe."

"She needs socks too," Anna piped in before pulling Dahlia into yet another room. This one was small and shaped oddly, all weird angles and stained glass windows. The furniture was old, definitely antique, and Anna nudged her to sit down in one of the fuzzy chairs. Willie flopped down right at her feet.

Mary quickly appeared and handed Dahlia a soft robe and big fuzzy socks. "You just put those on and warm up. The police have already arrived, so it won't be long before we know more."

It was then Dahlia noted the gun at Anna's hip. The way Mary had closed and locked the door.

They could act calm and cheerful, but this was serious. And somehow Dahlia felt...at fault for it all. Surely they'd been living completely normal lives before she'd hired them.

"I'm sorry this is happening. I... If I'd known it would cause so much trouble..." She trailed off, because what would she have done? Certainly not stopped looking for Rose and answers.

"Ms. Easton—Dahlia, this is what we do," Mary said. "We have processes in place to deal with this kind of thing because it's always the risk you run when you take on a case—cold or otherwise. We're all well trained to deal with threats. So, please, don't feel responsible for actions that aren't your own."

"Yeah, this is a piece of cake," Anna added.

The room fell into silence, and Dahlia had to look at the sisters. There wasn't much resemblance. Anna was more on the fair side, everything about her dress and demeanor screamed *tomboy*. Mary had darker hair and eyes and seemed all around more...prim.

It reminded her of her own sister. They each took after a different parent in looks and definitely had different personalities. Rose was so outgoing, so ready to try new things and dive into new experiences.

It still didn't make sense to Dahlia that she was the one doing *all* this. Rose was the tenacious one. Dahlia swallowed at the lump in her throat and focused on the stained glass window of a mountain with a big star at the top.

She wasn't sure how much time passed, but she put on the robe, the socks and warmed up a little.

Eventually there was a tap at the door, and Mary unlocked and opened it. Dahlia could hear Grant's voice, though he hadn't stepped in the room far enough for her to see him.

"The police arrested the guy. Jack will question him. For now, everyone can probably go back to sleep. There is just one…slight oddity to the whole thing. He's a kid."

"A *kid*?" Anna repeated.

"If I had to guess? I'd say not a day over sixteen." He stepped farther into the room, and Dahlia leapt to her feet, heart slamming into her ribcage.

"You're bleeding."

"Oh." Grant lifted a hand to his mouth and pulled it back, examining the blood. "Was a little shocked to find a kid, so he got a lucky shot in." Then Grant shrugged like it was nothing.

And his sisters kept throwing out questions like it didn't matter.

"But he wasn't armed?" Anna asked.

"Had a gun on him, but he didn't pull it. Can't say I know what to think about the whole thing. The police will do some investigating, make sure his prints match the others, and he's the only one, but—"

"You're *bleeding*," Dahlia interrupted, because she was still standing here, heart beating too hard, staring at the smudge of blood at the corner of his mouth. Didn't anyone, least of all *him*, care?

All three sets of eyes looked at her with varying amounts of consideration.

Then Mary smiled kindly. "I'll get something to clean it up." She stepped out of the room, Anna at her heels.

"Yeah, I'll help you."

So, it was just her and Grant alone in this strange room. In this strange new version of her life.

"I've had a lot worse than a busted lip from some kid," he offered, as if *that* were some kind of comfort. "You really don't need to worry about it."

Dahlia turned away from him, because no matter what he said, she just hated the sight of blood. Hated knowing—no matter how Anna or Mary acted—that this was about her.

She stared hard at that mountain of stained glass.

"Dahlia," Grant said, and it wasn't the way he usually spoke. All stiff orders and frustration. There was a note of softness he only usually deployed at those family dinners. He was also closer than he had been. "I can't tell you not to be afraid, but I can assure you that HSS will do everything to get to the bottom of this while keeping you safe."

She swallowed. She felt like spun glass. Like every time she got her footing in this terrible situation, some earthquake came along. She didn't want to be weak. She didn't want to cry.

She just wanted to find her sister. She cleared her throat, calling on every last piece of strength within her. "It's very disorienting. I guess I just need to find my footing." *Again*.

"You're doing just fine." He gave her shoulder a little squeeze. Friendly. Reassuring. But when he released her, his hand moved down her shoulder blade. It was a casual move, just the way a hand would fall off a shoulder as someone pulled it away.

But it twisted through her like something else and made her breath hitch.

He cleared his throat and created distance between them—almost as if he felt it too.

Clearly she was delusional. Sleep deprived. "I'm very tired."

"I'm sure you are. We'll keep an eye on the security cameras until we know for sure this kid acted alone, but you're fine to go back to your room and sleep."

She nodded as Anna and Mary came back in with a little first aid kit, smiling over something they'd said to each other in the hallway.

"You want me to take you back to your room?

All the hallways are confusing till you get used to it," Anna said.

"Sure. Thanks." Anna stepped back into the hall, and Dahlia followed, Willie always at her heels, but she found herself looking back at Grant, who was standing there letting Mary dab away the blood on his face.

He looked so…strong. Like some Western movie hero. A tiny bit beat up, but noble and true and right. *You're doing just fine.* It was the strangest thing. How easy it was to believe when *he* said it. Because he looked like he knew. Like all his convictions *had* to be right, or the world would crumble into dust.

But he didn't believe her about Truth or the Greens. Because he didn't want to, not because there wasn't evidence.

So he wasn't her friend. He wasn't her protector. He wasn't anything, except a man she paid to help.

But the way he'd touched her shoulder kept her awake for the rest of the night.

Chapter Nine

Grant never did get much sleep after that. What he wanted to do was head down to the sheriff's department immediately, but Jack would want everything on the up and up, which meant no HSS interference until later.

It worried Grant that the perpetrator was a minor. That parents or the juvenile detention center—when they didn't have a local one of those—would complicate getting answers.

But he did his chores, ate his breakfast and waited for Dahlia to emerge from her room. Once she did, he'd take her down to the police station and figure out if there was anything to go on.

The phone in his pocket began to ring as he walked back to the house from his second round of morning chores. The caller ID showed the library's number, and Grant hoped it would be Mrs. Riley with some information or lead now that she'd realized her reaction to the Green connection had been overboard.

"Hudson," Grant answered.

"Hi, Grant. It's Freya."

Grant winced. Good Lord, this was not what he needed. "Hi, Freya."

"I thought I should call you. I know you were working with that redhead yesterday, and Mrs. Riley wasn't very helpful."

"No, she wasn't." Grant stepped into the house, stamping his boots on mats meant to pick up all the ranch mud.

"Well, she was complaining to Mr. Durst about it this morning. About the Greens. Mr. Durst obviously pointed out that they're all dead and so on. But…"

"But?"

"I shouldn't stick my nose in this, I know, but the redhead was really nice. And I wanted to help. And…"

"What is it Freya?"

"Mrs. Riley said something about how she's connected to the Greens? Dahlia, right?"

"Very loosely, it seems. A century ago or something. All that genealogy stuff. You know how that goes. Turns out everyone's related half the time."

"Well, yes, but Mrs. Riley was talking about how the redheaded Greens were always the bad ones. She seemed so…angry, and it was just kind of weird. Even Mr. Durst told her she was being ridiculous."

Redheaded Greens? Eugene Green had been

bald and so had the man in that picture with Dahlia's sister. But there were other Greens. He didn't want to remember all the pictures of Truth in its heyday.

"Thanks, Freya. It's good to know that's what people are saying. Can you do me a favor?"

"Anything."

He winced at the fervor in her tone. "If the gossip mill starts winding up, will you do what you can to stop it? Or at least correct it. No one needs Mrs. Riley stirring people up into thinking this is some kind of direct connection to the Greens or Truth."

"Sure, Grant. I can do that."

"Thanks, I appreciate it."

"No problem. Anytime. Really."

"I'll see you around, Freya. Bye." He pressed End, feeling the way he always did. Uncomfortable, guilty. There was nothing wrong with Freya. She was a sweet woman. And, okay, he could admit he'd known she was going out with Palmer to see if *he'd* pay attention, but he just…wasn't interested.

He was complicated. And there was no point in throwing those complications out for everyone in town to know when they already talked about his family plenty.

Once his boots were clean, he left the mud room and went into the kitchen. Dahlia stood there alone, except for Willie at her feet, staring out the window over the sink. She held a mug of coffee but didn't seem to hear him enter.

The sunlight streamed in, making her red hair glow, like a flame. And then there were those blue eyes, lost and hurting, and he wanted to...

What the hell is wrong with you?

He should be thinking about Mrs. Riley assuming this was some kind of bad Green mark on her. The way Mrs. Riley spread gossip around town, everyone would believe it by the end of the day. Freya would try to turn the tide, but people loved a story.

He should know.

As if she finally sensed him there, she turned to look at him. She didn't register any surprise or discomfort at him just standing there *staring* at her.

"Do you know any more?" Dahlia asked without any kind of greeting.

"Not really. We can head down to the station whenever you want, confer with Jack."

She nodded. "I'd like to do that right away."

"Of course. But have you eaten anything?"

She looked down at the coffee, then made a face. "I really... I'm not a breakfast person. And it feels strange to..."

She trailed off as he began to open the pantry. He wasn't going to force a full meal on her, but he wasn't about to take her to the police station without something in her stomach. He found the variety pack of granola bars Anna loved so much and held out the box to her. "Pick one."

She hesitated.

He shook the box. "You feel better when you eat, don't you?"

She huffed out an irritated breath but then took one. "Happy?"

"I will be once you eat it."

This time she scrunched up her nose, but she opened the bar and took a bite. But she kept… staring at him.

It took him a few uncomfortable seconds to realize there was a *reason* her eyes kept drifting to his mouth. And they were none of the ones he'd been imagining.

It was because that's where he'd been bleeding last night. It wasn't even really swollen. There was just the little cut on his lip where the kid's elbow had knocked it into his tooth.

"I guess you're doing okay, then," she said after a few bites of granola bar.

"It was really nothing."

She nodded. "I just don't know how to make sense of it all. People don't get hit in my world. There aren't disappearances and stalkers and all this."

He didn't say the obvious. It *was* her world now, whether it made sense or not.

He also didn't say what he should tell her—that the town was going to look at her like the Devil now that Mrs. Riley undoubtedly shared a bunch of wrongheaded rumors. And unfortunately for Dahlia, her red hair wasn't any different than a big red A in this instance.

But maybe once they got to the bottom of whoever was watching her, she'd have enough answers to head back to Minnesota, and it wouldn't matter.

Why that thought settled so uncomfortably in his chest wasn't worth thinking about. "You want to grab anything before we head into town?"

She shook her head. "No, I'm ready."

DAHLIA FELT OKAY. More sturdy than not. She hadn't slept well, but whoever had been watching her had been caught, and it was both a relief and maybe a lead.

She desperately wanted a lead.

But when Grant pulled up in front of the sheriff's department, dread pooled in her stomach. Whoever had been watching her—a *teenager*—was in here.

"Jack will likely ask you a few questions. Hopefully he'll be able to give us some information to go on, but even if he doesn't, just the fact this guy is in custody is a new lead to follow."

Dahlia knew Grant was trying to assure her, so she attempted to smile and nod and feel reassured.

But she just kept thinking about how her sister was probably dead, and this *child,* essentially, might know something or be involved. There might be answers here, and for this entire year, the quest for them had driven her. Even knowing Rose might be—probably was—dead.

Faced with the possibility of confirmation…

"Dahlia," Grant said, with that rare gentleness that made her want to cry. "There's a reason my family specializes in cold cases. It's because they're unique. The way they drag out to the point where answers start to feel like as much of a curse as not knowing. We get it. So we can sit here as long as you need, or I can go in alone."

"It's just… I guess I never fully understood that an answer doesn't really change anything, does it?" She looked out the windshield, desperately trying to hold it all together. "If she's…gone, she's still gone. Whether I know or not."

Grant nodded along. "But you want to know. Or you would have given up a long time ago, Dahlia. A lot of people do."

She let out a shaky breath. He was right. Her parents had given up. Her and Rose's friends. Everyone had said *enough*, and she hadn't been able to. She sucked in a steadying breath. "Okay. I'm ready."

They both got out of the truck, and Grant met her at the front. He put his hand on her back and guided her inside. It was a friendly offer of support. Made all the more poignant by the fact everyone had...stopped offering that. Everyone wanted her to give up. Either be sad or get over it. Not stay mired in the what-ifs.

But Grant and his family understood. Dahlia hadn't realized how much she needed that. How much she missed feeling like someone...cared.

Of course, it was their job, and she was paying them, so it wasn't real care. But it still felt like a weight lifted.

He opened the door, and his hand stayed on her back as they entered. It was a small office, and the woman behind the desk looked up. She obviously knew Grant, but something odd flickered in her gaze when she took in Dahlia.

Still, she smiled and greeted Grant. "Your brother's back in the holding room."

Grant nodded and led Dahlia past the front desk. Jack was standing in a hallway and didn't greet them when he saw them, just nodded his head in a *follow me* gesture. So they did. Back to a little room with a big window. Jack pointed at the teenager inside, sitting next to a woman in a black suit.

"Do you know him?"

Dahlia swallowed and looked through the mirrored window. She studied the teen's face, desperate for any kind of recognition. And found none. "No."

Jack nodded as if that's what he'd expected. "Let's go into my office and have a chat."

He led them to the same small room she'd been in yesterday answering his questions. The same fat black cat slinked off the desk when Jack shooed it.

Jack Hudson did not seem like the type of man to care for a cat, but Dahlia hadn't asked questions then and didn't plan to now.

"Who is he?" she asked.

"His name is Kory Smithfield. Sixteen years old. A year and a half ago, he was reported missing by his parents in Austin, Texas."

Dahlia thought her knees might buckle, but she stiffened them and steadied herself by holding on to the back of a chair. She was afraid if she sat on it she'd never get back up. "Texas."

Jack nodded, his expression nothing but stoic. "We asked him some questions, talked to his parents. They can't come get him, and I didn't get the impression they were that interested in having him home at this point. We're going to have to send him to the juvenile center in Cody, at which point, finding answers is going to get complicated."

"Where's he been living since he went missing?" Grant asked.

"He wouldn't say. Pretended like he didn't run away, but it's clearly him. He also refused to admit he was following or watching Ms. Easton. Which is fine. We have proof. I'd like to bring Dahlia in to talk to him, but we'll need a lawyer present to make that aboveboard, and the parents weren't paying."

"So, what? It's a dead end?" Dahlia asked. Even though... Texas. If he was connected with Texas and had somehow wound up here in Wyoming...

He wasn't the man in the security footage with Rose, so maybe she was making too big of a leap to think it connected.

But it had to, didn't it?

"Not exactly." Jack paused, as if grappling with something significant. His cool gaze moved from Dahlia to his brother. "Grant, he has a tattoo."

She felt Grant stiffen next to her. Neither brother said anything, but their reaction made her think of her research, of all the things she'd read about the cult she was somehow connected to.

"He has an Order of Truth tattoo?" Dahlia demanded.

Grant scowled but said nothing. Jack didn't confirm, but *obviously* that's what it was.

"It connects. He *connects*. You can't deny it. You can't keep denying it. He was watching me. He has an Order of Truth *tattoo*. You have to let me talk to him. You have to let me ask him some questions. You *have*—"

"The only thing I *have* to do is follow the letter of the law," Jack replied stiffly. "I let you go in there, and the entire stalking case against you goes up in smoke."

"I don't care!"

"Dahlia."

She whirled on Grant. "I don't. I don't! He has something to do with my sister's disappearance. Maybe he killed her, and I don't care if he's sixteen or sixty. I will find out what happened to my sister. I *will*."

"Take a breath," he said gently.

But boy, that was the *wrong* thing to say. "Take a breath? This is the first hint of a lead I've had, and you're trying to stand in my way when I hired you all to *help*." She was not going to cry. She wasn't.

Grant put his hand on her shoulder. It should have infuriated her, but there was something about the heavy weight of a big hand and the serious way he looked at her. None of the dismissiveness she was used to from men and law enforcement.

He didn't say anything to her though, instead he moved that serious gaze to his brother. "We don't want to impact any potential case, but surely there's *some* way she can ask this kid a few questions. Or you could on her behalf."

"I've asked him plenty. He's not talking."

"Jack."

Dahlia didn't think Jack would relent. He was like a mountain. Absolutely no give. She expected that from Grant as well, but whatever passed between the brothers—something Dahlia didn't see or understand—had Jack blowing out a breath.

"I have to move him to a cell until we can transport him. Which means I'll have to walk him down the hallway. And there's no reason you couldn't…also be in the hallway."

What was she going to do with a hallway passing? She almost argued some more, but Grant looked back at her with a nod like *This is as good as it's going to get.*

Her mind scrambled for some idea as Jack moved back out of his office and to the holding room she'd looked into.

The teen still sat there looking calm. Maybe a little irritated, but not nervous. Not worried.

Dahlia couldn't imagine running away from home and then being picked up by the police and not being sad and scared.

"Stay here," Jack ordered. "Whatever you ask, whatever he says, it's completely inadmissible in a court of law. So just keep that in mind."

Grant's hand was on her back again, like he'd keep her there if necessary. Still, she didn't know what to say. What to ask. *Where is my sister? Why are you watching me?*

Jack went into the room, said something to the kid before he got to his feet. He was handcuffed, then Jack pulled him out of the room. Dahlia couldn't seem to find words, because the boy laughed and smiled like this was just a fun game.

"I didn't even know sheriffs were real. Sounds fake to me," the boy was saying. "Not good enough to be a real cop?"

Jack said nothing, but he met Dahlia's gaze over the teen's head. Which made the boy look over at her.

He looked at her, and while she saw nothing that made her feel like she knew him, there was something about the way he stared at her that made her feel...exposed. Like he knew exactly who *she* was.

Then he smiled at her, and her blood ran completely cold. She couldn't force *any* words out of her mouth.

He tried to lean forward, but Jack jerked him into place. Still, Dahlia heard exactly what the boy whispered.

"You'll be with your sister soon."

Chapter Ten

Grant didn't think the move through. He simply reacted. He reached out, meaning to get a hand on the kid, but Jack was faster, stepping between them. "He's going to a cell," Jack said icily.

When that little bastard had *threatened* Dahlia. Grant looked down at Dahlia. She'd gone white as a sheet, and no wonder.

"Dahlia." But he didn't know what to say.

She raised her blue eyes to his, looking a bit like a shell-shocked victim. "You heard him, right? You heard what he said."

Grant nodded. He wanted to say something reassuring, but he came up empty. The kid had mentioned Dahlia's sister without prompting. He had an Order of Truth tattoo.

Damn it.

"What do we do if we can't ask him questions? How do we get answers if Jack is all 'letter of the law' about this?" Dahlia demanded. Some of her color was coming back, so that was good.

But they weren't going to get anywhere with

Jack. Not when he thought he had a good case against the kid. Not when everything about this was going to stir up everything…*everything.* "I have my ways. Come on."

He got her out of the station before Jack was finished with the kid. Jack would no doubt want to lecture them on what they could and couldn't do.

Typically Jack's work as sheriff didn't interfere with the cases HSS worked because even amongst the suspicious missing persons, many of them committed suicide or died accidentally. The few murder cases they'd found and worked on had involved mostly dead people, so there was nothing active to put Jack in a complicated position with his job.

But this? Dahlia's sister's cold case disappearance now intersected with a current stalking case. That tied to the Order of Truth.

Damn. Damn. Damn.

This wasn't even about him being wrong. He could deal with that. What he couldn't—or didn't want to—deal with was the way this would, yet again, tear up his hometown. A town that had perhaps only in the past ten years started healing from what happened at Truth.

And it would bring up *everything* with his parents' disappearance once more. Grant didn't just dread it. He wasn't sure how he was going to *stand* it.

He unlocked his truck and waited for Dahlia to climb in. She was clutching her hands together, looking like she was about ready to jump out of her skin.

"We've got his name. Where he came from. The tattoo. It's a lot to go on," Grant offered, hoping to relax her some. He pulled out of the station parking lot with the thought of heading home. He and his siblings would all start researching Kory Smithfield ASAP.

And going down those old traumatic roads that led to the Order of Truth.

"What about that casing we found in Truth?" Dahlia asked.

"Jack's got that too, so he'll see if it matches the gun the kid had." But that was another thing that bothered Grant. When he'd wrestled that kid to the ground, the kid had tried to get away. But he hadn't tried to use his gun on Grant. He hadn't been a particularly adept fighter either. He hadn't wanted to be caught, but there'd been no thirst for violence in his reaction.

And yet, the smile he'd given Dahlia, the whispered words, they were *chilling*. As was the thought of that boy with that gun trailing around after Dahlia, watching her.

"The casing could tell us…something, right?"

He wouldn't say what he was thinking. Because unfortunately, without a body, even a murder weapon didn't mean much. But he tried to smile reassuringly at Dahlia. "It's definitely a lead of some kind."

"Wait. Stop," Dahlia said, reaching across and placing her hand on his over the steering wheel. She pointed at the library out his window as he slowed to a stop in the middle of Main Street. "I think we should go see Mrs. Riley. She said she made sure she knew all about the Greens. She might know if Eugene had sons, nephews, someone who looked like him. Maybe they aren't in Truth, but they're somewhere if that boy had a tattoo."

Grant hesitated. It was strange how much he wanted to protect her from the truth. Mostly he didn't mind being a little abrasively straightforward. But he supposed most of the people he dealt with were his siblings and ranch hands, so it suited the circumstances.

Dahlia was… Well, he didn't know how to explain it. She was soft, but she was strong. She was always on the verge of breaking apart but somehow always pulled it back together. And she was doing something he couldn't do anything but respect.

Finding answers for her family, no matter what it took.

So he didn't want to tell her Mrs. Riley wouldn't see her or answer her questions. That she'd likely already spread it around town that Dahlia was the next coming of cults and Greens and Truth nonsense. And the arrest of Kory Smithfield was only going to exacerbate the problem.

But apparently he didn't have to tell Dahlia any of that.

"I know she won't want to speak with me," Dahlia said earnestly, and her hand was still over his on the steering wheel. "But you could go talk to her. I could just…wait somewhere. Here in the truck or hang out in the library. I could go over to the general store if you think she'll see me and not talk. You go in and ask her questions, and I'll stay out of sight."

Grant wondered if even he could get through to Mrs. Riley since she knew Dahlia was his client, but he'd try. *After* he got her somewhere safe. "I'll take you back to the ranch and—"

"We don't have time for that."

They did have time—there was always time—but she had her first real lead in over a year. He understood why she wouldn't want to have patience now when, finally, it felt like something might move forward.

But she very clearly hadn't accepted the situation yet, or at least the implications as they connected to *her*. If she thought he was going to leave her alone for a second, she was *sorely* mistaken.

"Dahlia." He didn't want to be the one to put the thought in her head, though it was hard for him to understand how she hadn't arrived at the same conclusion yet. "What he said to you back there was a *threat*. Which means the possibility there is still someone out there who might want to cause you harm is high. You're not going to be out of my sight unless you're safe inside the ranch house until we know who else might be after you. And why."

IT WASN'T THAT Dahlia didn't understand what Grant was saying. Once he said it out loud, she went back over the whole experience and sort of…processed the situation. She'd been so focused on the sister part—the confirmation that boy knew something about Rose—she hadn't even fully grasped that her seeing Rose soon was…probably a death threat.

Rose was dead.

And she was sitting in some strange cowboy's truck in the middle of small-town Wyoming, thinking he could help her find answers.

Dahlia let out a slow breath and carefully sucked it in. She felt like she was on the verge of breaking into a million pieces, but she simply wouldn't let herself.

You're not going to be out of my sight unless you're safe inside the ranch house until we know who else might be after you. And why.

He wanted to help. He wanted, for whatever reason, to help keep her safe. He was worried. She knew it was business, not personal, but to be worried about her when it had nothing to do with her mental state felt…oddly like a huge weight had been lifted off her shoulders.

"But I agree with you," he continued when she didn't say anything. "Mrs. Riley might have more answers about the Greens still around and that might be a lead. I'm going to take you back to the ranch though."

Dahlia looked out of the passenger side window at the pretty little town and the sunny fall afternoon as Grant began to drive again. She had hired the Hudsons to look into this. Investigate. Find the connections. And here Grant was doing just that, all the while protecting her from a potential threat.

Going back to the ranch was what she should do. She was hardly going to *ignore* a death threat, but going through her binders in that beautiful room just made her feel like screaming. Which was ridiculous, because aside from a scenery change, that was about what she'd been doing for the past year. And now there was a *lead*. She should want to pore over everything again.

She turned to Grant, studying his profile while he drove. He was no different than Jack. An immovable mountain made up of certainty and strength of purpose. She wished she could emulate it.

Or get through to it. "Grant…" But she didn't have any experience laying out her feelings for people. She hated to ask for anything, hated to be seen as a burden. She *liked* being self-sufficient. She didn't mind being the one everyone forgot about, because that meant no one was paying too close attention to her.

Because when they did, they tended to think her strange or, since Rose disappeared, unhinged.

Grant spared her a glance, then his gaze dropped to where she realized she still had her hand rested atop his on the steering wheel.

She pulled it back and dropped it in her lap like it wasn't her own appendage. There was just something…comforting about him. She didn't know why. He was abrupt sometimes. She knew he tried to be gentle, but he wasn't especially *good* at it, even if she did appreciate the attempt.

"I know it's hard to sit around and wait. Or worry," Grant said. Because for all his inability to be gentle, he *did* have understanding. True understanding. In a way no one else in her life seemed to. Which was a comfort, Dahlia supposed.

"It's all I've done for a year, and now there's *finally* this…piece. I don't know how to fit it in, but it's a piece. He said, 'your sister.' He *knows* about Rose. I can't go back to the ranch and sit in that room and stew just because…"

"Just because he *threatened* you? That's not a *just* because in my world, Dahlia. It's a big damn *because*."

Dahlia sighed and looked away out the window as the landscape passed. Mountains and fall colors. Such a pretty place, and her sister had likely been murdered. For some reason, that runaway teenager thought she would be next.

She thought about the cranky woman at the library who'd immediately taken against her. That woman had said… "Mrs. Riley told us they would know about me. That they knew their tree backward and forward, and a loose connection wouldn't matter, it was still a connection. But if Eugene Green has been dead fifty years, who was she talking about in the here and now when she said, 'they?'"

Grant frowned at the road ahead of them. He clearly didn't like the connection to Truth or the Greens, but he was no longer trying to talk her out of it. "Listen, Mrs. Riley is…difficult. Her father joined the cult when she was a teenager. Her mom left her dad because she saw it for what it was, but the dad took some of the kids in there with them, and then… Well, her brother was one of the people who helped bring in the Feds. He always told her their father had tried to escape, but once you're initiated into the Order, you can't leave. Not alive anyway."

Dahlia listened to that reasoning. It explained some of the woman's animosity, she supposed.

"They all died. Her father, her brothers—the ones who were involved, the ones who tried to bring it down. The remaining Rileys have always… Well, they're bitter. Understandably."

"But they're also *knowledgeable*, Grant."

His jaw tightened, but he didn't argue with her. "We just have to be careful about how we approach her. It's a lot of trauma. All this happened before I was born, but for my entire childhood, it was such a…sore subject for everyone. It affected the whole town, generations of families. All of whom lost people."

He didn't say it, but she heard it all the same. *Just like you.*

He sighed before he continued. "And the thing is, this kid and his tattoo… It doesn't just stir up old, bad memories for people here. It means someone out there is still…" He shook his head. "I can't believe I'm saying this, but it means everything we thought *ended* back in 1978 didn't actually end. And that's going to hurt a lot of people."

"They've already been hurt. And so has my sister. Just because time has passed doesn't mean the hurt isn't still there. Surely you of all people know that."

"People want it to be over," Grant said stiffly.

"But it's *not*."

He spared her a glance, and she thought he was going to argue with her further, but instead he reached across the space between them abruptly. He pushed her head down, enough so that she let out a little yelp of pain. "Stay down," he ordered.

A second before something exploded.

Chapter Eleven

Grant kept one hand pushing Dahlia's head down away from the windows and one hand with a death grip on the steering wheel as the truck jerked beneath them.

Someone had shot out his tire. It was better than shooting Dahlia's *head*, but it still wasn't good.

He was halfway between town and the ranch, a stretch of highway that didn't see much traffic that wasn't a member of his family. Which meant this was very carefully planned and not good for either him or Dahlia.

He couldn't drive well on the flat tire, particularly in his best approximation of a crouch in the hopes that any other shots that went off didn't actually hit him or Dahlia. He had a gun, but it was locked in the glove compartment, and if he couldn't drive his way out of this, he supposed he'd have to shoot his way out.

Something uncomfortable and a lot like dread curled in his gut. He hadn't had much luck shooting since he'd come back from the Marines. The few times he'd sucked it up and forced himself to target practice, all his former accuracy and skill seemed to be completely and utterly gone.

So he'd stopped trying.

But now someone was shooting *at* him and Dahlia, and he was going to have to be able to do something about it. Whether his brain wanted to cooperate or not.

The truck was screeching metal now, tire rim against concrete at a bad angle that meant the whole thing could flip if he wasn't careful. Driving much longer like this was almost as dangerous as getting shot at.

So he slammed on the brakes, and Dahlia let out a little yelp as the seat belt kept her from slamming into the dash. He ripped the keys out of the ignition. "Keep your head down," he ordered, releasing her head and shoving the key into the hole on the glove compartment. He unlocked it, then scanned the world around them as he pulled his gun out.

He spotted the shooter in the rearview mirror—up on a ridge and working his way down it. But as far as Grant was concerned, that was the least of his problems. There were three other men moving out from various protected areas—moving to circle them.

He didn't have much time. And if there were

any more men hiding, they were probably in for a world of hurt.

But he didn't let his mind go down that road. He could only deal with the threat in front of him. He turned to Dahlia. "You're going to stay in the truck. Call 911. I'm going to take care of it."

"Take care of what?" she demanded, though she was definitely shaken, crouching there low enough her head wasn't visible in any of the windows.

But it was then a few things dawned on him. One, the shooter on the ridge hadn't shot again, though he could have. Two, the three men who were currently moving to surround the truck didn't appear to have weapons—not visible or drawn anyway.

Which meant this wasn't simply an attempt to murder Dahlia, or anyone looking into Rose's disappearance.

It was something else.

"Just stay put," Grant said, and then he had to trust she would. He opened the door, keeping the shooter behind him in sight. He waited to see if the man would lift the gun and aim it at him, but he simply kept moving down the ridge and toward the road.

Grant turned his attention back to the much closer men. Even if they didn't have visible guns, he didn't like the idea of them surrounding the truck. Even if they didn't want to kill anyone, nothing they wanted could be *good*.

"I think you fellas have the wrong people," he called out to the man closest—the one coming for the front of the truck, while the other two spread out to the east and the west respectively. He eyed the open door's side view mirror and saw the other man still climbing down the rock he'd been perched atop.

None of the men responded to him. They just kept advancing. Grant adjusted the grip on his gun, trying to focus on the goal rather than the anxiety clutching at his chest. He had to keep Dahlia safe.

Had to.

"Come any closer, and I'm going to have to start shooting," Grant warned. He aimed at the man in front. "We've called the cops, so why don't you all turn around? Go back where you came from."

They seemed wholly unafraid, though they didn't keep moving forward. The man in front studied Grant. "Is it true? Do you have her?"

Grant squeezed his hand in an attempt to keep it from going numb like the rest of his body seemed to be doing. "Who?" Grant said, and the three men answered in succession.

"The true one."

"The answer."

"Our promised."

Grant had seen a lot of terrible things. He'd been scared and freaked out more times than he liked to count. But this was possibly one of the creepiest damn things he'd ever encountered.

"That's not going to work for me. I warned you about taking another step."

But the man in front took one. So Grant got off a shot—aiming for a few feet in front of the forward-moving man. The shot went shorter and way wider than he'd anticipated.

He cursed under his breath. *Not now. Now when it matters.*

The men did stop advancing. They didn't turn around and run away or anything, but they stopped taking steps.

"Give us the woman," the man he'd shot at said in an authoritative tone. "And you'll be rewarded."

But there was something...familiar about him. The voice or the way the man in front stood. Grant moved toward him, gun still held and pointed at him. But the man didn't move or even eye the gun warily. He stood, chin held high, eyes on the truck as if he were trying to catch a glimpse of Dahlia.

Not going to happen.

It was when Grant got close enough to see the man's ear that it finally dawned on him who it was. "Lyle?"

"Lyle's dead," the man said flatly. But it *was*

Lyle Stuart. He'd been one of Jack's buddies in high school, but once Mom and Dad disappeared, Jack had cut ties because Lyle made trouble wherever he went. And Lyle was *always* recognizable because he was missing half his ear from a dog attack when he'd been a kid.

Lyle had left Sunrise years ago. Grant couldn't remember where he was supposed to have gone, but he did remember it was not long after Mom and Dad disappeared. Jack had said it was a good riddance type situation.

Now, all these years later, here Lyle was. Older, definitely having lived some hard years, but Lyle Stuart. Part of this damn cult that had somehow been revived.

And they wanted Dahlia.

"I've got some bad news for you, Lyle. Dead or alive, you're not getting her."

DAHLIA FOLLOWED INSTRUCTIONS for a while. She'd called 911, though it had been hard to give the dispatcher enough information. She didn't know enough about the area to give first responders an idea of where they were. The dispatcher kept asking her questions she didn't know the answers to.

"Jack Hudson will know where we are," she'd finally said. "The sheriff in Sunrise, Wyoming."

"Sunrise, Wyoming," the dispatcher repeated. "Stay on the line, miss."

Dahlia did, but she wasn't really paying attention to what the dispatcher said, because a loud *bang* exploded through the air. Dahlia dropped the phone and looked up over the dash, eyes frantically searching the area.

There was a man in front of the truck and two other men on either side of the truck. Grant was moving toward the man in front, but no one seemed hurt. Or scared. While her heart was racing and her palms were sweating.

Phone forgotten, everything forgotten except someone *shooting*, she watched as Grant stopped in front of the man who now stood in the middle of the road as if he were blocking the truck, when the truck was leaning at such an angle, she didn't have any reason to believe it *could* go.

It was almost like they were squared off. They were a good ten feet apart if not more, and they were talking, though she couldn't hear what they were saying. Grant had his gun pointed at the man, but the expressions on their faces weren't antagonistic, exactly.

More wary. Waiting. Considering.

She looked out the passenger window, then the opening left by Grant leaving the driver's side door open. The other two men were watching the exchange, though sometimes they would turn their gaze to the truck, and Dahlia would duck down—not sure why she felt like she didn't want them to even see her when they no doubt knew she was in the car.

She twisted in her seat, still crouched, and carefully poked her head up—inch by inch—until she could see out the back. A man stood there as well, gun pointed at Grant's back.

Dahlia did *not* like that.

But no one was immediately shooting. Still, she couldn't understand why Grant wasn't looking back, wasn't worried about the man with the gun. Surely he knew that man was there.

"Lord of Truth," the man in front of Grant yelled, raising his hands up to the sky. "Help us."

The two other men on either side of the truck began to do the same. They just kept shouting those words over and over, looking up at the sky like something might drop down and save them. Dahlia looked back at the man with the gun. He was moving again toward the truck. Toward her.

She knew this was about her just by the way the man looked at her through the back window of the truck. He was zeroed in on her, while the other men shouted about truth and help.

She wanted to cover her ears. It was only the voices of three men, but the repetitive words were so loud and alarming.

She heard the back door of the truck creak open, and she no longer saw the gunman in the windows. She looked wildly for Grant, but he was no longer standing off with the man in front, who was still chanting at the sky in time with the other men.

Maybe it was him. She looked back at the door, and a gun barrel appeared. "Get out of the truck," an unfamiliar voice said, though the face was hidden behind the door itself.

She didn't have anything to use as a weapon. Didn't know what to do except…refuse. "No," she replied as she looked around wildly. There had to be something she could use as defense, but as she looked to the right of her, she noticed one of the other men advancing toward the door.

It was locked, but that didn't make her feel safe, particularly since he was still yelling words about truth and help. She didn't *see* a gun, but that didn't mean he didn't have one.

Maybe this was what happened to Rose.

She looked back at the gun pointed at her. It was beyond surreal. Maybe it was not being able to see the man behind it, or how little experience she had with guns, but it was almost impossible to believe it could kill her.

But maybe it killed Rose. Could she convince this man to keep her alive and take her to wherever he'd taken Rose? Maybe she'd die, but maybe she'd know?

Before she could act on that irrational thought, the gun disappeared. She heard a distinctive male grunt and then a clattering sound. She scrambled over to the driver's side to see through the windows.

Grant was grappling with the gunman. He took

an elbow to the stomach but barely even winced as he pivoted and jabbed his fist up, hitting the man squarely in the jaw. The man stumbled back and into the truck on a grunt. Meanwhile the shouts from the other men continued to echo outside.

She thought maybe she heard sirens beyond all that noise and prayed help was on the way, because she didn't have the slightest idea what to do.

The gun. Guns. The man had been holding a gun and so had Grant, but where were they now? She peeked her head out of the doorway and saw them both on the ground. One right by the gunman's boot and the other a few yards away, almost in the ditch next to the roadway.

She didn't know how to use a gun, but if she got them both, she could give them to Grant. And none of these screaming men could get them.

She slid out of the truck and onto shaking legs, but she focused on the guns. She crept toward the one by the ditch because she didn't want to get in the way of Grant's grappling. Grant landed another punch, but the man refused to go down.

Dahlia took another shaking step toward the gun. She could do this. She could help. But she heard movement next to her, and when she turned, one of the yelling men was too close. No longer yelling. Just staring at her and *smiling*.

She wanted to bolt. Just start running and screaming in the opposite direction, but she was only two steps maybe away from the gun. She took another step, but he reached out.

She jumped away, but he never stopped smiling or advancing. He didn't lunge. He didn't speak. Just kept moving for her, arms outstretched.

"Don't move another muscle."

Dahlia froze in time with the man, because it was Grant's voice, low and lethal. When she got it through her head he was talking to the man—not her—she looked over at him.

He had a gun—not the one she'd been going for but presumably the original gunman's, who was crawling on the ground, gasping for breath as blood leaked out of his mouth.

Sirens sounded, and two police cars appeared on the rise. The man next to her and the other shouting man ran. Back from wherever they'd come, still shouting about truth and gifts.

Dahlia took a few halting steps after them. They might know who killed Rose. They might have answers.

"Dahlia."

She looked at Grant and realized he, too, was bleeding. Like…badly. The entire bottom of his shirt was slowly becoming soaked with blood, and it was his *own*. It was then she saw in the hand that didn't hold a gun, he held a knife. Covered in blood.

Her stomach threatened to roil. "Grant," she said, not knowing what else to say. He'd been *stabbed.* She moved haltingly for him, but she had no idea how to fix a stab wound.

The police were coming. She could hear them shouting now as they approached, guns drawn. She looked around, but the man who'd been crawling was gone. *Gone.*

And Grant was bleeding and… She had to do something. Something. But Jack ran over.

"About damn time," Grant muttered.

"He's hurt. He's… He needs an ambulance," Dahlia babbled at Jack, whose face went from worried to a blank kind of coolness Dahlia couldn't believe. Grant was his *brother.*

He started talking into a com unit. Barking out orders as he put his hand on Grant's shoulder.

His face betrayed nothing, but there was a slight shake to his hand as he placed it there.

"The men. They…they tried to… You have to follow them."

Jack's gaze turned to hers. It cooled even more. "We'll handle it."

"I'm fine," Grant said, but he didn't sound himself, and he still hadn't moved. The gun was still pointed where the man had been. He still held the dripping knife. He still bled.

But another officer came running. He held a little white box Dahlia assumed was a first aid kit.

"Why don't you get out of the way," Jack said to her. "Take a seat in one of the cruisers. We'll have questions for you once we take care of Grant."

Dahlia wanted to argue. To *help*. But Jack moved in such a way that he blocked her view of Grant, and he spoke with the other officer in quiet tones she couldn't make out.

Dismissed. No, ordered away. Jack clearly blamed *her* for what had happened, and was he wrong? She'd cowered in that truck, and then even when she'd finally attempted to do something, Grant—bleeding—had been the one to stop the man from getting her.

She backed away from Jack. From Grant. She blinked a few times as she shakily moved for the cruisers still flashing lights though the sirens were off. The men who'd stopped Grant's truck, all gone.

Had any officers followed those men? Maybe she should just run after them. They wanted her. Why not go see why? Better than…this horrible feeling of uselessness and guilt.

But another person arrived, this time in a truck just like Grant's. Mary and Anna got out, and while Anna made a beeline for Jack and Grant, Mary came right for Dahlia.

"Are you okay?" She reached out and took Dahlia by the elbows so that she had to focus on Mary rather than Jack blocking her from Grant or the men who'd run off into the rocks and ridges.

"Grant…"

"They'll take him to the hospital, and I'll take you home. He's fine. Standing on his own two feet, right?" She slid her arm around Dahlia's waist and began leading Dahlia to the truck. Dahlia watched over her shoulder, but between Jack, Anna and the other deputy, she couldn't actually see Grant.

She turned her attention to where the men had gone. "The police..."

"They'll see if they can find who tried to hurt you and get answers," Mary said, giving her a reassuring squeeze and delivering her to the passenger side of the truck.

"But they didn't try to hurt me," Dahlia said, turning to look at Mary. That man had been close, but even when he'd tried to take her arm, it hadn't been violent. He'd been *smiling*. Grant was the one they'd fought. The one they'd hurt.

Mary looked back at her for a long minute. "Dahlia, maybe they didn't physically hurt you, but that doesn't mean they didn't hurt you in other ways." She opened the passenger door. "Get in now. We'll sort it all out back at the ranch."

She didn't want to leave Grant. Or this place that felt like maybe it had answers to Rose's disappearance.

But Mary smiled and squeezed her elbows again. "Dahlia, we're going to help. But there's nothing more to be done in the middle of the road."

We're going to help. They hadn't given up. They'd found something, and Grant had protected her. This was more forward movement than she'd had the entire thirteen months Rose had been gone. She should be happy, excited that there were real leads to follow.

So why did she just want to cry. She swallowed at the lump in her throat. "Are you sure he's okay?" she asked on a whisper.

"If he wasn't, I'd be over there. Go on now. Get in the truck."

So Dahlia finally did.

Chapter Twelve

"I'm fine," Grant said to his older brother. Perhaps for the three hundredth time. He didn't know why he was saying it. It wouldn't ever get through Jack's hard head. He glanced in the rearview mirror at his sister sitting in the back as the cruiser sped toward the hospital with lights and sirens going. He wouldn't get through her hard head either.

A very annoying Hudson trait.

"You were stabbed," Jack said through gritted teeth, every part of his body so tense Grant was pretty sure if he reached out and poked Jack, he'd shatter into a million pieces.

Tempting. But the throbbing pain in his stomach kept him from doing much moving. "Yeah, better than shot," he muttered. He adjusted in the chair, then hissed out a breath. It still pissed him off that guy had managed to stick him with that knife, but his focus *had* been on the gun and getting it away from being pointed at Dahlia. But this was a flesh wound at most.

"They wanted to kidnap her." Grant stared hard at the road that would lead them to the hospital. Where he'd get poked and prodded and stitched up and no doubt sent home in a few hours' time. He felt a little sick at the prospect of *hospitals*. But that was hardly the only thing bothering him. "They were chanting all this crazy stuff about *truth*. Lyle Stuart—and I *know* it was Lyle—said, and I quote, 'Lyle's dead.' This is real cult stuff. And they want Dahlia. They called her 'the answer.' 'The promised' or something. She's the target, and *she's* in danger."

"Yeah, and you're the one bleeding through your bandage."

Grant didn't even bother to look down at said bandage. Paying more attention to all the ways he hurt wasn't going to help. "Did you send any deputies after them?"

Jack flicked a glance at him, his hands flexing on the steering wheel. "I only had one to spare."

Grant stared open-mouthed at Jack for a good minute before speaking again. "Damn it all to hell, Jack. What were you thinking?"

"That I didn't want you or any of my deputies to die?"

"I'm not about to die from a flesh wound. And furthermore—"

"Furthermore, Deputy Brink tracked them for a bit. I've instructed her to put together a search party. They'll comb the area and get some leads.

We're certainly not going to let any Order of Truth copycats wreak havoc on our town."

Grant would have preferred to have been part of that search party rather than on his way to any hospital, but at least Jack had sent a team.

Then his brother went and ruined that *at least*. "I think we should back off this."

Grant looked back at Anna, even though it hurt, because if he reacted to his brother's flat-out *absurdity*, it wouldn't be pretty. "Please tell me he's kidding."

Anna looked at Jack, then Grant, as if deciding which side to take. Because Anna was never scared of taking a side. Or making up her own. But she kept her gaze on Jack. "So, what you're suggesting is we back off. Let that woman get taken by some unhinged cult, or copycat cult, and probably be killed just like her sister?"

"That is *not* what I'm suggesting," Jack replied darkly. He pulled to a stop at the ER entrance and switched off his sirens and lights. "We'll discuss it later."

Grant wanted to argue, but he also wanted his infuriating stab wound stitched up so he could stop bleeding through bandages. He didn't want to end up worse for the wear because of how much blood he'd lost.

So he got out of the car before Anna could help him, which made Jack growl. Grant didn't feel the least bit chagrined. His brother was being an overbearing jerk.

Not unusual.

Anna came up behind him and linked arms with him. "He's just shaken because you're hurt. It feels like a failure, so he'll be grumpy, but you know as well as I do he's not going to let that poor woman dance in the wind. Besides, Chloe's the one he put in charge of the search team, and you know she'll be thorough."

Chloe Brink was a fine cop, but… "I should be out there."

Anna shook her head. "Like hell you should."

They walked into the hospital and talked to the ER attendant, and then after what felt like hours, Grant was through all the rigmarole of being admitted and waiting for someone to come stitch him up.

The entire time, he replayed the moments in his head. What he could have, or should have, done differently. What all this meant for Dahlia. "They wanted her," he muttered to Anna.

She looked up from her phone. "Yeah, but they stabbed you."

"Which proves just how dangerous they are."

Anna shrugged.

The doctor came in and stitched him up, telling him how lucky he was and how he needed to take it easy and—*blah, blah, blah*. As if sensing an unresponsive patient, the doctor handed Anna the recovery instructions and the prescription for pain medication Grant had no plans on taking.

Then Anna started talking about horses with the doctor, the young man clearly flirting with her. She laid on the charm and flirted right back. Once the doctor *finally* left, saying they could too, Grant glared at his sister.

"Really? I've been *stabbed* and you're flirting with the doctor?"

"He was cute," Anna said with a grin.

They walked back out of the hospital. Everything in him kind of throbbed, but he'd rather feel the pain than be all zapped out on painkillers.

Been there, done that, no repeat performance, thanks.

Jack was in the parking lot pacing next to his cruiser, his phone to his ear.

"Uh-oh," Anna muttered. "Bad Jack vibes."

"Are there good Jack vibes?"

"Good point," she said with a laugh.

Jack ended his phone call as they approached. He studied Grant in silence for a few moments before he seemed satisfied Grant wasn't going to just keel over. "So?"

"Doctor says he'll be fine," Anna said because Grant knew Jack wouldn't believe *his* recounting of what the doctor said. "Needs to rest, but it didn't hit anything important."

Jack nodded. "That's good news. Unfortunately I have some of the bad kind."

"Of course you do," Anna said.

"The man who stabbed you? They caught up with him pretty easily…because he was dead."

"Dead?"

"Shot in the head."

Grant was…stunned. "I didn't…"

"No, but someone did. And left him there while they disappeared. Seemingly into thin air."

Grant had to bite his tongue to keep from telling his brother he should have handled things differently. It wasn't fair. Jack had more to worry about than getting to the bottom of this—the safety of his citizens and deputies chief among them.

But Grant should have gone after them himself, stab wound be damned.

"This situation is too dangerous," Jack said, relying heavily on the "I may be your brother, but I was also your father more or less" tone that Grant hated. *Hated.* It was that tone that had sent him to the Marines, at least partially. "We're turning it *all* over to law enforcement. The case. The woman. Beginning and end of story."

Grant didn't say anything to Jack, because it was pointless. Like talking to a brick wall or worse.

But like hell this was the end.

DAHLIA REALLY COULDN'T get over the kindness of Mary. Not only did the woman make her lunch and insist she eat, but she also seemed to understand what Dahlia needed even when Dahlia couldn't articulate it.

She didn't insist Dahlia rest. Instead she brightly suggested Dahlia help with some of Mary's administrative tasks. They were simple—filing mostly—but it helped ease some of that useless feeling and kept her mind engaged enough not to fall apart, but not so engaged she actually had to *think*.

When the phone rang, Dahlia jerked in surprise. She'd been reliving those moments on the road over and over again, trying to work out what she should have done differently as she'd filed the stack of papers Mary had given her.

Mary answered the phone, and Dahlia shamelessly listened in. At first Mary sounded businesslike, then relieved. "Okay. Yes. Yes." There was a flicker of something. Her cheerful demeanor slipping for just a moment. "All right. I'll tell her. Uh-huh. See you soon."

Mary smiled brightly as she hung up the phone and turned to Dahlia at the filing cabinet. "Grant's all stitched up and on his way home. Good to go. He'll be back in the saddle in no time."

But there was something else. Something bad. Dahlia sucked in a breath, bracing herself for… She didn't know what.

"Unfortunately, the deputies couldn't find the men who stopped you guys."

"Oh."

"At least right away." Mary reached out and put a gentle hand on her arm. "I'm sure they'll discover clues to help them search, and this is a concrete crime for them to investigate."

Still, Dahlia got the feeling there was more to it, and Mary was purposefully keeping it from her. She wished she knew Mary better so she could demand whatever information. But at the end of the day, Mary wasn't her friend. She was just part of the organization Dahlia was paying to help find her sister.

And now things were…complicated. Because there was an *active* crime, and the police were involved, and she was somehow…a target in all this.

She wasn't going to ask what Mary was keeping to herself. It didn't feel right in the moment. But that didn't mean she couldn't start…being active. Making some of her own decisions.

Since Grant had found her poking around Truth, the Hudsons had taken over, and she'd let them. She couldn't let that continue. Not with Grant hurt. Not knowing she was some kind of bizarre cult target for whatever reason.

So, she focused on what she knew how to do. What she *could* do. "Mary, do you have anything about the Order of Truth? When I was doing my research, I focused on Eugene Green and his family more than the cult itself. Maybe I need to learn more about this cult."

Mary hesitated, which seemed a rare thing for the woman who was always very composed. "I'm not sure..."

"I can't just sit around. I..." She couldn't explain what she felt to Mary, or she'd end up crying. "I have to do something. And the only thing I'm any good at is research."

Mary nodded as if she understood not just what Dahlia was saying but, on a deeper level, what it meant. "Jack and Grant never wanted anything about the cult around. It was a leftover reaction from my parents. We weren't allowed to talk about it growing up or even joke about it. You see—" Mary waved it away "—it has always been a very sore subject in our house, and Jack and Grant were the oldest, so they took it to heart the most."

Dahlia understood there was more to that story but also that it was none of her business. "I guess I could just do some internet searching," Dahlia said, thinking aloud.

"Oh, don't do that. There's so much bad information. People love to sensationalize a cult. Just...stay here for a second."

Mary disappeared and Dahlia waited, then went ahead and finished filing. It gave her hands something to do. It gave her mind some sense of accomplishment.

When Mary returned, it was with a stack of books. "I'm not sure how Anna's going to feel about this, but I wanted to get them to you before Jack and Grant get back. Maybe it's part and parcel with being the youngest and how little she remembers of my parents, but Anna's always been obsessed with the cult business against the rest of our wishes. These are all hers. If she kept these, they have better information than you'll find on the internet. I promise."

She handed the books off, and Dahlia took them. The top title was *Order of Truth: Fact and Fiction.*

"Take them to your room. Keep them out of sight if you think Grant might be in there. I'll let Anna know you have them, and if she has an issue with that, we'll figure it out."

"Thank you," Dahlia said, even though what she really wanted to say was *Why would Grant be in my room?* "I think I'll go do some reading then. Can you…" She trailed off. She'd see Grant at dinner, and Mary had assured her he was fine multiple times, but still, she just…wanted to see for herself. But for some reason the comment about Grant and her room made this all feel…awkward. "If you ever need more help with things, it makes me feel useful."

Especially since, at most, she could afford maybe another week of their services and their generosity. She needed answers and she needed them quick. So she moved through the maze of a house to her room.

When she got there, she shut the door behind her and looked through the titles. When she'd been researching before coming to Sunrise, it had been all about Eugene Green and how he connected to her, to Texas, to Truth. So, she'd learned some things about the Order of Truth, but not really the inner workings, the beliefs and all that. It hadn't seemed pertinent. Because everything was about genealogy and blood connections.

But the men had been...chanting, reaching for the sky. It had to be some kind of...ritual? Or something related to the cult. She flipped through indexes, trying to determine what kind of information she wanted.

Not the raid or the murders. She wasn't ready to delve into all that. But what did the group believe? What was *their* truth?

Lord of Truth! Help us! They'd shouted.

So, who was this Lord? She found a chapter in one of the books titled "Lord of Truth" and began to read. It didn't seem to be based on any religion she was familiar with. It was a mix of things—nature and signs, but mostly the bottom line seemed to be Eugene Green himself.

He was the Lord of Truth. Only Eugene and his descendants knew the truth.

Dahlia felt a cold chill run through her at the word *descendants*. She wasn't a direct descendent of Eugene Green and neither was Rose, so it made no sense that these men wanted her.

But Mrs. Riley had said they would know their tree. They would know about her.

But maybe that was only part of it. Maybe it was *Rose* knowing about them.

A knock sounded at the door and Dahlia jumped a foot. She looked around a little wildly and realized she'd been reading for some time now. The light outside was dim instead of bright afternoon.

"Dahlia?"

It was Grant's voice. She wanted to throw open the door, see for herself he was all right. But Mary's warning about Grant not seeing the books had her grabbing them all and shoving them frantically under the bed. "Just a minute!"

It was ridiculous. Like she was a child sneaking Harry Potter again when her parents didn't approve. But she supposed as much as she wanted it to be different because she was an adult, it wasn't, because this was Grant and his family's house.

Not hers.

She tried to steady her uneven breathing and the odd nerves that moved through her. She wanted to *see* he was all right, and she didn't want to face what had happened.

But it was time she stopped being such a coward.

She opened the door and tried to manage her

best approximation of a smile. He stood there looking just as he had this morning. Maybe he was a little pale, but he stood on his own two feet and didn't seem to hold himself any differently.

He was fine and whole.

"I just wanted to make sure you're all right," he said, his eyes warm and kind.

"Me? You're the one who was hurt." She wanted to reach out and touch him. Assure herself he was as real and sturdy as he seemed. But there was all this space between them, and it felt like some kind of wall.

"I'm sorry," he offered stiffly.

But she couldn't fathom what he was apologizing for.

"For what?"

"They got away. Now Jack's got a crime to investigate, and he will—him and his department—do an excellent job."

"I wish I found that convincing."

He pulled a face. "I wish I could feel more convincing, but the truth is their hands are tied by the law in a way mine aren't. I won't be giving up on this, Dahlia. I want you to know that. I won't rest until we find who's after you. And I am not bound to the laws Jack is."

He said it so earnestly. Like it was a vow or a promise. Like her safety was important to him personally. Like he'd protect her.

"I'm not sure anyone has ever..." She trailed

off, because it was a foolish thing to say, to feel. She was *paying* him, and she couldn't keep doing it for much longer. So she needed to figure out how to protect herself. "Grant, I need you to do something for me."

"What?"

"I need you to teach me to fight."

Chapter Thirteen

Grant found himself at a loss for words. She looked a little healthier than she had when she'd first come to them, but she was still on the frail side. She was a librarian and tended toward skittish. She'd told him herself she wasn't athletic. He just…couldn't picture her throwing a punch.

But anyone could learn—that or how to shoot a gun. Anna had always taken to shooting and fighting, but it had been Mary's natural inclination to avoid those things, and still she'd learned. Grant considered her marksmanship a personal triumph. He had taught her, after all.

Before you lost the ability.

"I can see what you're thinking," Dahlia said, sounding *almost* peeved. "And you aren't wrong. I'm weak. I don't know the first thing about protecting myself, except to walk with my keys between my fingers in a dark parking lot, but that's just it. I spent my whole life avoiding the dark parking lot. The sketchy situation. I can't avoid this. And I *hate* what happened today. Not just because you were hurt but because I just sat there and let it happen. I hate the fact I hid and didn't know what to do. I was *weak*."

"You went for the gun. You didn't hide. The fact that you're here, still standing, after all you've been through, isn't weakness."

But she was having none of it. "I did hide for a while, and I only went to the gun to keep it from them. I don't know what to do with a gun. And if they're going to keep coming after me, I should know how to fight or shoot or something."

"I'm going to be here." He had to resist the urge to take her by the shoulders. To press all of his assurances into her like he could tattoo them on her. "We're all going to be here protecting you."

"Not forever," she replied, clearly troubled.

He didn't know why it bothered him that she was already thinking ahead to that. He didn't know why he wanted to…just protect her. When his sisters had been growing up, he'd been all about giving them the skills to protect themselves.

Nothing about his reaction to Dahlia ever made any sense. But she *was* speaking logically, even if something deep inside him rebelled at the thought. "We can do that. Teach you some self-defense."

She let out a breath as if she'd been afraid he'd refuse the request. "Thank you." Then she took a step forward, hesitated. But seemed to sort of gather herself, or her courage, and reach out. She put a hand on his arm and looked him right in the eye. "I'm so sorry you were hurt."

It was such a genuine flat-out apology—something that had not existed in his life as a Hudson or in his life as a Marine. He could only stare back at her. What did someone *say* to that? Who just came out and apologized with no equivocations or attempts to pick a fight?

She cleared her throat and let her hand drop, which felt like a loss. For a moment it was like he was reconnected to some old pieces of himself he'd thought he'd lost.

Which was a particularly ridiculous thought. "I've survived worse."

Her eyebrows drew together, and he forgot that people who weren't military or his family didn't always have that same dark sense of humor or slightly warped way of looking at things.

"Were you hurt in the military?"

Grant shrugged. "Here and there. Nothing major. Never sent me home over it."

This did not assuage her concern or smooth out the furrow in her brow. "Is that why you don't like talking about it?"

There was something about her blue eyes, the way she looked at him that felt like looking *into* him. He'd swear she was hypnotizing him if he believed in such things.

"I survived my injuries. No, I don't see the

need to recount them, but they don't weigh on me. They are what they are."

"Then what does weigh on you?"

If anyone else had asked that question, he would have tensed. He would have barked out a rebuff as a response or said nothing at all. *Anyone* else.

But it was Dahlia, and she was just…different. And open. She had no preconceived opinions about him. No opinions on his military experience or what he wore to the tenth grade homecoming. She apologized and stumbled in the mud and loved dogs. She had her own demons, and somehow…that made him want to share his own.

"I was lucky. Not everyone was. Not just… making it home in one piece but being able to bear the weight of what you see."

Her hand rubbed up and down his elbow for a second. Comfort, or an attempt at it. "I'm not sure I'm bearing the weight of anything very well lately," she said, her voice quiet. Sad.

He couldn't help himself. He lifted his own hand and rested it over hers on his elbow. He smoothed his thumb over the top of her hand. "Not all weights are meant to be borne easily. Certainly not loss and grief. Those are the weights you have to learn to carry in whatever ways you can. You've come this far, Dahlia. And I am intimately acquainted with the strength you need to push forward when everyone tells you to let it go. Jack and the family… We may not have gotten our answers, but we stuck it out a lot longer than anyone else. We exhausted every option. I'm proud of that, and it made the weight easier to carry eventually."

Her hand was small and warm, the skin soft where his thumb brushed. For a moment her eyes dropped to their joined hands, and he saw the little hitch in her breath and felt something he really wasn't allowed to feel when it came to a client.

Maybe it wasn't a Hudson rule, but it damn well should be.

She looked up then, pinning him with that blue gaze. "I know you said you're not a war hero, but why do people *think* you're one?"

It was enough of an uncomfortable and unwanted topic that he managed to pull his hand away instead of getting lost deeper in this moment that was feeling more and more dangerous.

"Why are we having this conversation?" he asked. "We'll be late for dinner."

"Right." She looked away and attempted to smile as her hand dropped off his arm, but it faltered. "Sorry. I'm not usually nosy."

"So, why are you now?"

"I…don't know."

"Can I be nosy for a second?"

She sucked in a breath and let it out like she was preparing herself. When she looked at him again, she had her pleasant but distant smile on. "Sure."

He shouldn't ask. He should keep his big mouth shut. It was one hundred percent none of his business. She was a client, and regardless of her answer, it changed nothing. And still the words came out anyway. "There's no one waiting for you back home?"

"Well, my parents, but they're not really waiting for me."

"That's...not what I meant."

Confusion lined her face, but then she seemed to clue in. If the blush creeping into her cheeks was anything to go by.

"Oh. No. There's...no one."

Grant should maybe laugh it off or say something about needing to know for safety reasons or something ridiculous. But he didn't. "Ready for dinner?" he asked instead.

And she nodded and followed him out of the room.

DAHLIA HAD GONE through dinner wondering if Grant had used some sort of...distraction tactic on her. Flirt with the mess of a woman wanting to learn to fight, and she'll forget all about it.

Or something.

But the next morning at breakfast, Anna and Palmer were waiting for her. "Grant said you wanted to learn some self-defense." So he'd listened. And done something about her request.

"Oh, well, yes." She tried not to look around the kitchen and into the big dining room and failed. "Is he around?"

"I sent him back to bed. He looked *terrible*." As if realizing this was the wrong thing to say to the woman who felt slightly responsible for his *stab* wound, Anna quickly continued on. "That was at like five this morning. He's refusing to take the pain meds, so he just didn't sleep well. I bet he'll be back down any minute for some breakfast. Everything else is just fine on the Grant front."

"That seems generous, Anna," Palmer said, clearly teasing as he earned himself a glare from his sister. Then a hard jab to the stomach that had Palmer doubling over a little.

"The element of surprise is your first lesson," Anna said, back to smiling. "That and eat a solid breakfast." They all turned as they heard a noise—Grant entering the kitchen.

Dahlia didn't think he looked terrible, but he hadn't shaved or combed his hair, so he did look a little dangerously disheveled. It made her stomach do little flips. She didn't even *know* this man, not really, and her silly immature reaction to him was really starting to be a problem.

"How's it going, champ?" Palmer greeted.

"Just fantastic," Grant grumbled. But he looked

over at Dahlia and managed a smile, if a little gruff around the edges. "Morning."

"Good morning," she replied. "I could make—"

"Mary already made you two plates," Anna interrupted, pulling the refrigerator door open. "She said you're both on the 'on the mend' diet. Lots of protein and liquids."

"I'm not injured," Dahlia protested.

"No, but you're *way* too skinny, and Mary loves to mother. She's on horse duty this morning, but she instructed me by threat of pain and suffering to warm up your meals and make sure you eat." Anna popped one plate into the microwave as she said this. "Go on into the dining room. I live to serve."

Palmer gave an exaggerated laugh. "That's a new one."

Still, Grant and Palmer moved into the dining room, so Dahlia felt like she had to as well. She took a seat in the chair that seemed to be *hers*, while Palmer and Grant spoke of some ranch thing and sipped their coffee.

Anna entered soon enough, carrying two plates she set in front of Dahlia and Grant. "Eat up or face the wrath of Mary, a surprisingly alarming force if provoked."

Dahlia tried to smile. Her appetite hadn't returned any on its own, but the food was always so delicious once she started, she'd manage to eat the whole meal. Maybe she was learning to feed her body even when it seemed to not want to be fed.

"We'll go over some basic protection moves and how to use a gun," Palmer said, as if this were a normal thing to discuss over breakfast. So casual. "Anna and I will show you the self-defense moves since Grant has to rest, but he'll teach you how to shoot."

"Maybe she'd do better with a female teacher," Grant offered, shifting in his chair, then wincing. Dahlia wished there was anything she could do to take the pain away.

"Or someone more on par with a beginner's skills," Palmer said, clearly teasing Anna.

But Anna didn't seem interested in rising to the bait. "Grant's the best shot, by far. And he's the most patient out of any of us, but Mary or I can do it if you want."

"Hey, I can be patient," Palmer replied.

"Yeah, getting out of bed maybe," Anna grumbled.

"I don't really…" Dahlia swallowed. She wanted their help so badly, had even asked Grant for it, but it seemed like too much. "I appreciate—"

"Dahlia," Grant interrupted. "You need to stop thinking you're some kind of burden to us."

She looked at him, arrested by how simply he cut to the heart of the matter when she wasn't sure she'd even realized that was the clearest verbalization of her thoughts.

"But..." She'd always felt...a bit like a burden to everyone. And she'd worked very hard to shrink herself down, shut herself out, so no one thought she took up too much space or asked for too much.

Rose's disappearance had been an odd turning point in her life, giving her a courage and determination she'd never had. So maybe it required a change in how she looked at the world around her.

Not a burden but a person who took an opportunity when it was offered.

"This whole thing is to help people," Anna said, gesturing around the house. "Because we've been there. So, no burdens."

"It has to be a business," Palmer continued. "Realistically. But that doesn't mean it isn't more than that too."

"There's a reason we keep a running ranch along with it," Grant added. "That's about money and legacy. This is about...us."

"Trust me, the three of us? We don't offer *anything* out of the goodness of our hearts," Anna said.

Dahlia found herself glancing at Grant. He didn't argue with Anna, but Dahlia felt like he should have. He'd been *stabbed* in an effort to keep her safe. *That* was goodness.

"Eat," Grant told her gently. And she didn't know what else to do but that.

Chapter Fourteen

The days passed with very little forward movement. They kept Dahlia on the ranch, watched over by someone or cameras or a dog at all times. In the mornings, Grant or one of his siblings worked on her with either self-defense or shooting.

Jack's sheriff's department found nothing. It frustrated Grant, but when he was being fair, he realized that whatever kind of copycat group this was had been avoiding detection for some time, so just because law enforcement *knew* of them didn't mean it would make them easy to find.

If the group had really found Rose Easton and murdered her, as seemed likely, they'd spent over a year keeping everything under wraps—from law enforcement, private investigators and Dahlia herself.

Much as he didn't *want* to, Grant knew he needed to go back to Truth and poke around. The police had done it multiple times, but Grant just got the feeling there was something more there. And if not…well, at least it felt like *doing* something.

Because teaching Dahlia how to shoot was slow torture in the "this woman is very off-limits to me right now" department. And the very uncomfortable realization that the man he'd been before he'd been deployed would not have cared and done something about it anyway.

He found her with Anna in the little gym they had in one of the outbuildings. They were both breathing a little heavily, likely having been at self-defense practice for a half hour or so.

He didn't dare show up sooner, because watching her learn to punch and block and break holds should *not* have affected him in any way, but it did.

"Dead Eye is here," Anna announced cheerfully when she caught sight of him. "Just in time. I've got a few calls to take." Anna walked over to him, lowered her voice as she passed. "I'm going to be scarce for a few days, FYI."

"Am I the only one you're telling?"

"You and Mary," she replied, then flashed him a grin. "Don't go telling big brother on me. I know a guy who knows a guy. Might be able to get me some info. Might not. I'll be back by the weekend."

He resisted the urge to lecture Anna on being careful. He couldn't say they were alike in many ways, but while Jack, Palmer *and* Cash all wanted to lock her up in a room and pretend like she was still a little girl, Grant understood the restlessness. The need to get out there and take some risks.

But he was still himself and a man and a big brother. "Be careful."

"I was born careful," she replied. Which was a flat-out lie, but there was no use in arguing the point with her. He let her go instead. Just like all his siblings had let him go once upon a time.

When she was gone, he turned to Dahlia. She was standing a little uncertainly on one of the mats. Her gaze was on the gun in his hand, but she raised her eyes and forced a smile.

"I really appreciate—" At his scowl, she waved him off, but she smiled, and this one was genuine, not forced. She had the sweetest smile, not saccharine or anything. Just sort of like they were rare and special when she doled one out.

"It's not a *thank you* this time. Promise," she said. She gave the gun another sideways glance. She'd learned the safety rules and shot it a few times, but she didn't care for the noise or impact.

Dahlia approached him, and he got the impression she was trying to choose the right words to say. She was always so careful with her words, and he had to wonder what had made her that way.

"I appreciate you teaching me how to use it."

Then her shoulders drooped and she let out a really long sigh. "I just really hate it."

It was his turn to smile. "Yeah, I can tell."

She wrinkled her nose. "I know I'm a weakling."

"Hardly. Mary's not a fan either. She learned because it's a necessity out here, and it helped put Jack's mind at ease, but she's no fan. Cash won't touch guns around Izzy. They aren't toys. It's okay to be uneasy about them. Better than liking them *too* much."

She nodded. "I appreciate that. So, we could be done with this side of things since I could at least hold one and point it at somebody if I had to?" she asked hopefully.

"And we'll work really hard to make sure you don't have to," Grant said firmly. He'd make it his mission.

Her smile was back, though it wobbled a bit. "Um. The thing is. We've settled in. We've regrouped. I've got...very minimal self-defense skills, sure, but I have to *do* something. I'm running out of money, and before you tell me yet again the money doesn't matter, try to understand it matters to *me*."

He didn't *like* that it did, but he could understand it anyway. Pride and that need to feel like she had some control over her life. Still, he didn't need to dwell on the fact if she ran out of money, she'd leave.

"I was thinking about heading out to Truth this afternoon," he offered instead, though he hadn't really planned on telling her.

But he could admit, here in the privacy of his own mind, he wanted to spend time with her. Even if it was torture. It was the kind that reminded him not everything had broken irreparably in the Middle East.

"Jack won't approve, which means if you want to come, it'd just be us. And Willie. And we'll probably have to lie to my siblings. At least some of them. So you could tag along, as long as none of that bothers you."

She chewed on her bottom lip, and since he didn't want to look at *that* and let his mind wander, he looked at the curls around her temple that had fallen out of the hair tie she had most of her hair pulled back in.

"Well…" she began, not meeting his gaze "…speaking of lying."

Grant didn't need to feign surprise. "*You've* been lying?"

She looked up at him through her lashes. "It's not so much lying as omitting some facts you may not care for." She tried for a reassuring smile. "It's just, those chants really bothered me, and it pointed out a small hole in my research."

"What kind of hole?"

"I'd researched the Greens, how they connected to my family and what the cult *was*, sure, but not really the actual beliefs or rituals."

Grant usually had a good poker face, but nope, not when it came to the Order of Truth. "You've been researching the cult." It sat in his gut like a weight.

Dahlia looked pained. "Mary mentioned you wouldn't like that."

It frustrated him. That Dahlia looked guilty when she had every right to do whatever the hell she wanted. That his sister was going around discussing anything to do with the cult or his feelings on it with *anyone*. "Oh, Mary did, did she? And who else knows this is what you've been up to?"

"Well—" she blew out a breath "—I am sorry. Anna knows too, but that's it. We've kind of been discussing it, and I just—I *am* sorry. I know it bothers you, but I kept thinking that if maybe I understood…what they thought, what they did, it would give us some clue as to where they were or…" She reached out, just a light finger brush against the sleeve of his coat. "I *am* sorry."

"You don't owe me any apologies for doing what you think is best." Not that he could agree, even if she *was* right. His father had always warned him Truth was dangerous. Because it wasn't just about murderers and religious zealotry. It was about taking advantage of people desperate for something to believe in. Something to belong to.

He didn't think Dahlia was desperate, but she was alone. The few things she'd said about her family didn't paint a close picture. She was here in a place where she didn't really know anyone, trying to find her sister's *murderer*. It wasn't that he thought she was susceptible for falling for a cult. It was just all so dangerous and she had so very little support.

"I don't want you to be mad at me," she said when the silence between them stretched out.

"I'm not," he said, automatically. Being mad at her didn't have anything to do with what he was feeling. He hesitated to tell her the truth. "It's dangerous business. I know you don't need me to tell you that. It's just, I'm not even sure I can explain it. Truth has always been a shadow in this town, a boogeyman of sorts. I don't know anyone whose family wasn't affected, even if it was generations ago. My own parents included, and it was just…we were raised with the belief you don't go poking into Truth. It's an open wound." He sighed. "Anna, of course, loves poking at an open wound."

Her mouth curved very little, as if she agreed with his assessment of Anna, but she sobered quickly. "I don't want to poke at anything. I just want to find out what happened to my sister."

"I know. That's why even if I'm uncomfortable, I can't be angry with you."

"So, if you're all frowny and gruff, it's discomfort, not disapproval."

"Frowny and gruff? I think you've been spending too much time with my sisters."

She smiled a little, some of the gravity leaving her expression. He wished it would lighten any of the weight inside of him.

"It's a dangerous situation in a lot of ways. Particularly if we're wading into a murder investigation. Even if I understand, even if I even think it's a necessary step, poking into the Order of Truth is dangerous. And tricky. I worry about you."

Her eyes widened a little. "No one ever worries about me."

"Well, you can't say that, because I do."

She looked up at him, expression perfectly serious, but searching too. He didn't know what she was searching for. Didn't know if he wanted to give whatever it was if he could.

"Do you worry about everyone you help solve cold cases for?" she asked after a long pause, her voice quieter. More hushed.

He shook his head. "No." He could elaborate on that. Explain how his cases were rarely murders or dangerous, and never had to do with psychotic cults. But he didn't.

So they simply stood staring at each other. There was more he should say or a subject to change or something. His gaze certainly shouldn't drop to her mouth, and his body *definitely* shouldn't lean forward like she was some magnetic force he was pulled to.

But she didn't step back. She didn't break his gaze or do anything to *stop* him. He could have kissed her, easy enough. But the moment stretched too long, got too big in his head. And a loud, sharp bark interrupted any forward progress he'd thought of making.

Willie ran in, tail wagging, so it wasn't any kind of warning bark. Just an excited one. Grant looked at his watch. Had to, instead of risking a glance at her. Noon.

Grant cleared her throat. "That's the lunchtime signal."

"Right. Sure. So, lunch and then we'll go out to Truth…without telling anyone?"

Grant nodded. And felt, not at all for the first time, that he'd never get used to the man he'd become after leaving the military and returning home.

DAHLIA FOLLOWED GRANT INSIDE, and they ate lunch with Mary and Palmer. Then Grant encouraged her to grab a bag and any of her notes she thought might be helpful, and then they headed out to his truck to drive to Truth, Willie at her heels.

It was a strange and probably terrible thing

that she was thinking more about the way Grant had looked at her in the gym than she was about her notes and what she might want to investigate once they got to Truth.

She should be thinking about Rose. About murder and danger and wondering why knowing Rose was dead didn't bring her any sense of closure.

But she thought about the way Grant's eyes had moved to her mouth. The way he'd seemed... closer. The way no matter how she told herself she was probably hallucinating, it had seemed like he'd at least *considered* kissing her.

She was a terrible person. At least, that's what she kept trying to convince herself. But somewhere on the quiet drive over to Truth, she had the realization the voice in her head arguing with the trajectory of her thoughts sounded an awful lot like her mother.

Grant had said he *worried* about her, which was hard to fathom when her whole life she'd been told no one really *had* to worry about her. She was a good girl, who followed the rules and would never dream of stepping out of line. So what was there to worry about?

Rose had been the wild one. *And look where that got her.*

Again, her mother's voice. Not her own. If she had a friend in the exact position she was, would she be telling her friend she was a terrible person for thinking about more than just her sister? Or would she remind that friend that tragedy or not, she was still alive.

And for the first time in a long time, the thought felt like an optimistic one.

It wasn't just Grant and the possibility that he might inexplicably be interested in her. It was his whole family. The way they treated her more like family than her own did.

He was *worried* about her safety. She wanted to play it off like…it was just his noble heart. All that military stuff and wanting to help and protect people.

But it felt different, Grant's worry, than anything the rest of his family did. Even if they were nice and compassionate, the way Grant looked at her *was* different.

And your sister is dead.

But you are alive.

She snuck a look at Grant. His gaze was on the road ahead, and he looked so serious. There was a way his siblings treated him, and the kind of indulgent look he gave them when they did, that made her think he hadn't always been quite so stoic. Like maybe the military had hardened him.

But he was hardly all tough outer exterior. There was a softness underneath it all. Or maybe that wasn't the right word. Something hidden.

Willie stuck his head between the front two seats, pushing his nose against her shoulder until she twisted around to give his ears a scratch. "I've always wanted a dog," she said absently.

"Why don't you get one?"

"Oh, both my father and Rose are—were allergic. Then when I was on my own, my apartment didn't allow pets."

He seemed to think that over. "I don't want to tell you what to do, but at some point you've got to realize you're the adult and get to make the choices in your life for you, not other people. And I only say that because it was a strange realization I had when I got out of the military."

"I don't think you can compare leaving home and going to *war*."

He shrugged. "Depends, I guess, on how much your childhood felt like a war zone. Metaphorically."

She wanted to keep arguing with him, but it was the word *metaphorically* that kept the words lodged in her throat. Metaphorically, it had been a bit like a war. Her parents forever throwing volleys at Rose, and Rose forever hurling them right back. And Dahlia somewhere in the middle just trying to hide.

Grant didn't say any more, but he pulled his truck off the highway and onto the country road that led to Truth. Dahlia watched the landscape, and even though she knew the men that had stopped them in the road, the men who'd killed

Rose could be out there, she felt that same strange sense of peace as they came up on the ghost town.

She knew she was supposed to be appalled because of what had happened here, but… "It's such a pretty place."

He pulled the truck to a stop, and she could *feel* his disapproval, even if he didn't say it out loud.

"I know you can't look past what you know happened here, but there's something peaceful about it."

"You don't have to justify your feelings to me, Dahlia. You get to feel what you want. Kinda like you get to make the choices you want."

He started getting out of the truck, but she felt stuck for a moment. He didn't sound mad or dismissive, just like it was obvious. *You get to feel what you want.*

It was…revolutionary. Maybe because she'd led such a small life, but she was used to…defending herself at every turn. To always feeling like the odd man out who had to change what she thought or felt to suit everyone else. To stop all that metaphorical war.

He came around to her side of the truck and opened the door for her. But there was concern in his expression. "You okay?"

She swallowed. Sure, she was fine. Just having her whole worldview upended since the disappearance of her sister. "Yeah." She forced herself to get out of the truck, and Willie jumped out after her.

They stood there, shoulder to shoulder, surveying the abandoned town of Truth. Dahlia felt lost. For so long, the simple act of finding Rose had given her a goal. Something to fight for and toward.

She still wanted to find Rose's killer—she really did—but the confirmation she had to be dead was…disorienting.

And then Grant pointing out all these things she didn't *have* to do. All these old thought patterns and behaviors that didn't suit her.

Who *was* she?

Grant's hand covered hers, his fingers threading through hers. A gesture of support. He gave a little squeeze. Reassurance.

"Come on. Let's go poke around," he said.

Maybe she didn't know who she was anymore, or maybe she'd never known. Maybe she'd always been afraid. But she'd spent the last year doing the unthinkable, leading to this moment where she was holding hands with a handsome cowboy, determined to find answers.

So, she'd figure it out. She'd figure it *all* out.

Chapter Fifteen

Grant didn't know what he was looking for, but that often happened with cold cases—even ones that got a little warm. You had to look and be open for anything.

Even holding hands with your off-limits client.

It was meant to be a comforting gesture, and he felt like it had worked. But it was…more to him. Like reaching out and forging a connection when he'd spent the last year at home struggling to make connections.

She had such strength in her, but she still seemed a little reluctant to use it. He was getting the impression it came from a childhood of shrinking herself into a mold that didn't fit, and he knew…

His parents had been wonderful, but losing them the way they had, had put him and all his siblings in a kind of box. A mold they were expected to fill, and it had chafed, so he'd gone off to war.

And lost who he was.

Not the time. At all. They were here to find clues, not make some kind of large-scale realizations about life.

But he didn't let her hand go. She seemed to need that connection to move forward, and he didn't mind it himself. It took his mind off the throbbing pain in his side where the damned stab wound never stopped reminding him he'd been hurt.

"Remember that place where we found the bullet thing?" Dahlia asked.

"The casing, yes."

"I was reading, and that was like a holy place where they did rituals and things. Maybe they still do. Maybe that's why a casing was there."

"Do their rituals involve guns? Because even last week on the highway, only one of them had a gun and was using it."

"No. That is something I noticed about a lot of the literature. They don't believe in modern weapons. Though there was a whole section on how Eugene Green stockpiled semiautomatic weapons in a bunker. So, I guess it's your typical 'do what I say, not what I do.'"

Grant nodded grimly, and they walked through the alley and into the enclosed area. It didn't surprise him they did rituals there. It had always given him the creeps, the way the stone seemed to block out everything except the sky. Making you a target.

He didn't particularly want to go back in there, but they *had* found the casing there. So someone had been around. Maybe they'd just been doing target practice, maybe it had been kids, but maybe…there were more clues to be found.

She hesitated at the opening to the enclosed courtyard, which made him feel good about his own pause.

"They chose this place and built these walls because they said it was sacred ground containing some stones that were found here."

Grant looked at the dirt beneath his feet. "They didn't leave the stones?"

"No, they made them a kind of traveling altar for the Truth Prophet. As much as they settled here, there's this sense they always knew they had to be…mobile? Or nomads? Kind of like they needed to cling to this idea of being persecuted."

"Truth Prophet. Who listens to that garbage?"

Dahlia moved forward, and their fingers slid apart. She dropped his hand. "Desperate people do desperate things."

He felt chastised, though he didn't know why. He'd probably seen a lot more people do a lot more desperate things than she ever had. But she moved forward into the walled courtyard. The afternoon sun was high above lighting up the odd shadowed circle of earth and her with it.

The sun gleamed on her red hair. She looked like some kind of goddess. Ancient and powerful. He couldn't paint, couldn't take a picture in focus to save his life, but he somehow wanted to memorialize that moment where she looked…otherworldly and somehow perfectly at home. Here.

Perfect.

She looked away from the walls to him, then frowned. "What is it?" she asked.

"You're beautiful."

She opened her mouth, then closed it, clearly flustered. Part of him thought he should apologize. It wasn't *appropriate*. But it was true, so he didn't know how to pull it back.

She swallowed, visibly, looking up at him with those big blue eyes. Willie wagging his tail between them, as if he were an eager onlooker.

"Well, um. Thanks," she finally said when he couldn't quite come up with the right collection of words.

Grant shrugged. "Just true," he managed. Then he looked around the courtyard. "We found the shell casing right there," he said, pointing. "Was there anything about this place in particular in the books? Like it's special beyond sacred or…"

She shook her head. "Some things were specific, but they were more generic about where things happened. They never named Truth as their town or any of the waterways or mountains they considered sacred, just some of the things they did there. They didn't even specify this place, except that it was a stone circle and sacred because of what was found in the earth. Maybe there's another one somewhere too, but I figured since we knew this one existed, it was probably the one they were talking about."

Grant nodded along. He didn't understand adult people falling for this hocus pocus, sacred and prophets and what have you. Sure, a kid might be predisposed into whatever worship they were brought up in, but people choosing this… It made no sense to him.

Dahlia still stood in the center, squinting up at the sun now. "One thing the books all agreed on was the Truth Prophet is always a Green. They believe in blood and genetic ties. Sort of like the monarchy, but it's more about who's…powerful or connected to the truth, I guess."

He could see that she felt…bad about that. Like somehow she was connected to all this idiocy when she'd never stepped foot here before this month.

"You're not a Green."

She looked over at him. "No, but they want me for some reason." She seemed to grapple with telling him something. He found he didn't want to press. Whatever was on her mind, he wanted her to tell him of her own volition.

You have a real problem.

"They believe in sacrificing people. I think that's what they did here."

The word sacrifice gave him a cold chill, and

he could tell it bothered her too. Though even without studying, he knew the Order of Truth believed in human sacrifice. It was part of why they'd been such a story. "None of their so-called sacrifices were done with a bullet."

"No, they weren't," Dahlia agreed. She moved around the courtyard, Willie at her heels. She looked so alone. Like the world was on her shoulders, and Grant knew what that felt like. It didn't matter if people wanted to help you when you felt like there was some wall between you and the people. A wall you didn't know how to tear down or cross or ask for help through.

So, he followed her path around the area, wishing every step didn't cause a spiking pain through his stomach. But it was better than being numb on painkillers. He kept following her path until he was behind her as she studied the ground where they'd found the mysterious casing.

"Dahlia, what's on your mind? Hopefully you know that even if I don't agree, you can tell me. It doesn't change anything." Because he sensed that reluctance in her, and he couldn't help but wonder if she'd been talking to Mary or Anna about it, she would have just said it.

He didn't want to be the reason she didn't speak her mind. Didn't make suggestions.

She turned to face him, chewing on her bottom lip. She looked up at the sun again, then down at Willie. "Rose is blond," she said at length.

"Okay."

"The Greens who are the prophets? They always had red hair. It was a kind of…symbol."

He saw now what she was grappling with. It pained him that she could even think that connected her. "Dahlia, you're not a Green."

"Does it matter if I know I'm not if they think I am? I wasn't into it the way Rose was, but genes are science. It's DNA and chromosomes and… Does me having Green blood change who I am? No. But it makes me someone important to them."

It was why they wanted her. Why they'd been willing to hurt him but not her.

"Grant…" She looked up at him imploringly. Like she needed him to be on her side, and he had a very bad feeling he wouldn't want to be. "I think I need to let them take me."

DAHLIA KNEW HE wouldn't *agree* with the idea, but she hadn't expected him to laugh. She frowned at him as he laughed and laughed.

Then he seemed to get some dust in his nose and sneezed. He winced and kind of doubled over, clearly in pain from the whole thing.

And maybe it served him right for laughing, but she still felt bad. Especially when he let out a quiet string of curses, still bent over.

"Are you okay?" She reached out, hand on his shoulder, one on his jaw, needing to offer some comfort. Maybe it was his own fault for laughing, but she still felt at least partially responsible for his *stab* wound.

He straightened, tilted his head back and breathed deeply, but still winced because that likely hurt too.

"Guess I deserved that," he muttered. Then he reached up and patted her hand that was still on his jaw. But she didn't drop her hand, and then he just sort of left his there.

They stared at each other for the longest time, and she knew this was…secondary. Whatever they were starting to feel for one another didn't belong in a creepy cult, deserted ghost town on the search for her dead sister.

But it was something good in a sea of all that had been bad, and she wanted to cling to it like a life jacket. She could feel what she wanted. She could *do* what she wanted. She wasn't beholden to everyone else.

So when he took her hand off his jaw, she wanted to protest. Until he pulled it toward his mouth. He pressed his lips to her palm, holding her gaze the whole time. She would have said it was offhanded, but it *wasn't*. Because his mouth had touched her skin and that wasn't something friends just *did*. Certainly no friends she'd ever had.

He opened his mouth, and she braced herself for some apology or explanation. But instead of saying something that would make her feel foolish or angry, he closed his mouth.

Instead of excuses or walking away or letting Willie or anything distract him, like what had happened back in the gym, he leaned down and gently placed his mouth to hers.

And it was gentle, but it wasn't timid. It was careful, but he wasn't holding back. There was a sweetness to it and a heat. A deep longing sense of something inside of her clicking into place. Like this moment was exactly where she belonged.

When he eased away, it wasn't so much like an ending, but more like the natural ebb and flow of something. Come together, step apart. *Don't let go.*

And still she had no words, because that kiss was better than anything she'd ever read about. Any movie she'd sighed over. Maybe because it wasn't just fuzzy feelings of "wouldn't that be amazing?" Maybe it was just…reality was better than imagination.

With the right kind of man, anyway.

She looked up at him, not sure she understood the expression on his face. Maybe because it reflected so many things deep under the stoic mask she knew was more habit than who he was.

He was real and human and flawed, and so was she, and…she didn't know how this could happen in the middle of the worst year of her life. But that only seemed to make it more precious.

"Probably not the place for this." He didn't let her go, exactly. He smoothed his hand down her arm, then eased away, but not completely. Not like distance.

"Probably not."

He let out a long careful sigh. "I can't let you be taken, Dahlia. I get it. Why you'd think that'd be a solution. I'm not sure I wouldn't think the same thing in your position. But self-sacrifice isn't the answer here."

"Then what is?"

"I don't know. Sometimes it takes a while to find an answer. But I can't let anything happen to you. Professionally. Personally."

She felt a little flutter of panic because this was not expected. This was not what she'd come here for. Could a kiss change the course of her life? She very much wanted to see if it could. When she never, ever got what she wanted. Not really. "We don't even know each other," she said, her voice little more than a whisper.

"I wish I could agree with you. But you feel right, Dahlia."

It took her breath away. Probably because she knew he didn't say things he didn't mean. Because he wasn't prone to exaggeration or sparing feelings. If there was anything she was sure of when it came to Grant, it was that the truth was as sacred to him as this place had been to the cult that wanted her.

But if they took her, she could find answers. And if they didn't want her dead because of dumb things like bloodlines and red hair, didn't that mean she had some power in the situation?

He lifted her chin with his fingertips, forcing her to look him in the eye. "It isn't an option. I need you to promise me you understand that."

She decided to use his own words against him. "I wish I could agree with you and promise you that."

He frowned, but he didn't drop her chin. He didn't step away, and she realized she'd braced herself for him to do just that. And it wasn't fair. At every turn, Grant had not done what he wanted at the expense of what she wanted. He'd listened, considered, and even when he'd disagreed, it hadn't changed how he treated her, how he looked at her.

How he kissed her.

It was hard to know what to do with that when her agreement with everyone had always been the condition to their love.

"Okay," he said at last, his fingers still gently pressed to her chin. But his eyes darted to the left, and everything about him tensed, though he stood completely still. When he moved, it was a blur and he moved her with him.

He had her pressed up against the wall, the

stone cold against her back, him hard and warm against her front. It might be enjoyable if he wasn't looking at the top of the wall, if their bodies being pressed together was about that kiss earlier and not about him shielding her body with his.

"Grant."

"I heard something," he murmured. "We're definitely not alone. And this place is too open."

She realized he had his gun in one hand while another wrapped around her elbow like he was about to guide her somewhere.

"We'll move carefully out of here." He glanced at Willie, who was standing guard at the entrance. If he sensed anyone, he didn't show it, except in maybe the fact his tail wasn't wagging. But he didn't bark or growl.

"They want me, and not dead, maybe I should be the one protecting you," Dahlia said, worrying over his stab wound.

Grant's expression got even harder. "Just because they want you alive at first doesn't mean they always will. Keep that in mind before you go sacrificing yourself to your sister's memory."

It hurt, she supposed because it poked at a truth, and what she *had* been thinking. That she'd be safe even if it was scary. But maybe Rose had thought that too. Maybe a cult full of psychopaths and sociopaths only had so much use for a person, even if they were a redheaded descendent of a Green.

"I'll apologize for that later," he muttered irritably, taking her elbow. He moved her, always keeping his body sort of wrapped around hers, her back against the wall. Protecting her.

She knew he'd do it to anyone. It was who he was—a protector, a hero. But still, even though it wasn't personal to *her*, it was still something that made her heart stumble. That and even though he'd been harsh, which was just his natural way of things, he admitted the need to apologize.

They reached the opening of the courtyard, and Willie came to attention while Grant looked out, surveying the area presumably for people. "I don't see anyone, but someone is out there."

Dahlia remembered how she'd felt the last time she'd been here. In the end, she'd chalked up that feeling of being watched to the dog and Grant, but maybe there was more. Maybe someone was *always* here.

But they'd looked through the town and found no sign of people, and maybe she wouldn't know what signs to look for, but Grant would.

"Come on," he said, gently moving her out of the courtyard and into the alley, still blocking her as best he could.

They made it to the road when Willie let out a low growl, and Grant turned toward where the dog was focused, but Dahlia felt drawn to look to the right instead. Down the length of the abandoned street.

There was a figure in one of the broken windows. A shadow or…a person. She opened her mouth to tell Grant, but she caught the flash of something familiar. She stood stock still for longer than she could count. Surely it was a dream. A hallucination. She'd finally had that psychotic break her parents were so worried about.

But the figure didn't vanish. It moved from the window to the empty doorway. The figure— the person—appeared as real as anything else. "Rose," she whispered.

Just as Grant whirled around and shot.

Chapter Sixteen

Dahlia's scream echoed in Grant's ears even as he pushed her onto the ground. The man on the ridge disappeared, so Grant didn't think his shot had been in time. But he was ready for a return volley.

Dahlia struggled against him.

"Stay down. Someone could shoot back," he ordered.

"It's her," Dahlia said, still struggling.

Willie trembled next to her—not in fear, but because the dog was eager to track down the threat. But Grant could hardly leave Dahlia here without protection. So Willie had to stay.

Why did you bring her?

More screams echoed in his head, but he knew they weren't real. Or at least real in this moment. Old screams. Old smoke and explosions.

He really did not need this now.

"It's her. I saw her. Grant, I saw her," Dahlia kept saying. But he couldn't get his brain to click in. "Why'd you shoot at her?"

Lincoln is down. Get out of here, Hudson.

He squeezed his eyes shut against the old voices. He hadn't run. At least there was that. In the moment he could have saved himself, he hadn't. Unfortunately, his attempts to save his superior officer had been in vain.

"Grant?"

"Yeah," he said, or tried to say. It seemed to come out dry and dusty like the desert. But he opened his eyes. Focused on Dahlia. At some point, Dahlia had stopped struggling against his hold but shifted in it so she could look at him.

"What is it?" He could see the concern on her face and knew he had to put the past behind him. But it wrapped around him like a fist, a vision he couldn't shake.

"There was a man on the ridge over there," he said. Because he wasn't about to tell her what was going on in his mind, and he had to focus on the important facts for now. "He ran away, but he could circle around."

"What about Rose?"

He took a deep breath, using all those coping mechanisms the discharge therapist taught him. Breathe. Visualize. Ground himself. But it was hard when he also knew they were in danger. He couldn't compartmentalize the way he should with a gun in his hand, a current threat and old pain. "What about Rose?"

"I saw her. She was in that building." Dahlia pointed down the street.

Grant kept breathing carefully. He stared at the building, trying to ascertain if anything he saw was real or just old fragmented memories.

"I know I saw her. I know I did," Dahlia was saying. So insistent, like she thought he didn't believe her when he couldn't even work up the concentration to believe her or not.

"I thought you shot at her, but…" Dahlia trailed off, he thought. Or maybe he tuned her out.

Then he felt her fingers on his cheek, sort of like before. When he'd kissed her. He *had* kissed her. That had happened. All this was real. *She* was real.

"Grant, what's wrong?"

She looked so concerned, and he knew he had to get it together. They could still be in danger. Just like the highway. They wanted her. And Grant didn't think they particularly cared what happened to him in the process of that. His only saving grace was they didn't seem to be big on the use of guns.

He sucked in one more careful breath and let it out, hoping she'd keep her fingers right there on his face, which helped him do all that grounding he was supposed to do when he had an *episode*.

"You think you saw Rose in that building down there?" he said, hoping his voice sounded as calm to her as it did to him. Not matching what was rioting around inside of him at all.

"I *know* I saw her. At first, I thought I was hallucinating or something, but she moved. From the window to the door. And she was wearing this sweater that I gave her for her birthday a few years ago. It's got all these crazy flowers on it. I found it in a thrift shop, and I knew it was perfect for her."

"Okay. Okay." He tried to give her a reassuring smile. "She was in that building. And there was a man up on that ridge." And he hadn't shot him, because damn if Grant could hit a target these days.

He should have sent Dahlia here with Palmer or Jack or even Anna. Why did he think he could protect her when, very clearly, he couldn't? Couldn't save anyone. Not his parents. Not his sergeant.

Not going to make it, Hudson. Tell the wife I tried.

It had been the worst moment of his life, and this seemed to echo it in all the ways he couldn't allow.

"You have to let me go find her," Dahlia said, her hand still on his face, but she tried to tug her arm out of his grasp.

"It could be a trap," Grant said, not letting her go. She'd take off, and then what? They had to…

think this through. Calmly. Rationally. Which meant he had to find his equilibrium. Now.

Her expression turned, and he recognized desperation when he saw it. The need to *do* outweighing common sense. Been there. Done that.

"She could need help," Dahlia insisted, and she sounded so desperate. He could hardly keep holding her here. He didn't want to hurt her. And as much as his instincts shouted at him to get her out of here, were his instincts even any good anymore? Sure, he could shoot at a perceived threat, but he couldn't hit it. He could fight off men and still get stabbed in the process.

Now is not the time for some kind of identity crisis. It wasn't his own voice. He wasn't sure if it sounded more like his father or Sergeant Lincoln, or maybe some imaginary mixture of them both. Regardless of where the thought came from or who it sounded like, he needed to hold on to it.

"We need to get out of here. It isn't safe."

"I can't leave her behind," Dahlia said stubbornly. "Grant, I *know* I saw her. She's alive. She's *here*."

There were tears in her eyes, and if he had to blame his weakness on something, he supposed it was that. On wanting to give Dahlia…the world. "All right. We'll check it out. But you stay behind me. You follow orders. Got it?"

She nodded emphatically.

He should have let her go, moved away from

her hand on his face. He should have confronted all the danger around them and come up with a plan. Instead, he pulled her up to standing and pressed his mouth to her forehead. For her comfort. For his.

He just…needed to.

"Promise me. No self-sacrifice," he said, holding her there against him as she leaned into him.

She hesitated, but after a moment, she nodded.

"Out loud, Dahlia."

She let out a hefty sigh and pulled back a little. "Fine. I promise. Can we go find her now?"

It was Grant's turn to sigh. Most of the old visions and voices were gone now. He felt more in charge of the moment and himself. Not that he was particularly sturdy with it.

He turned, keeping his body as a kind of shield between anywhere someone might be and Dahlia. He studied the area. It was too open. Too many places for someone to hide.

He wanted to try to talk her out of it, but if he put himself in her shoes, he knew there'd be no words. If he'd sworn he'd seen his parents down there, wouldn't he do everything no matter the danger to get to them?

"Follow me. Don't look down at the store, watch behind us. Let me know if you see anything, and I mean *anything* that doesn't look right, feel right, whatever. We are basically sitting ducks walking down this street." Once they crossed, they'd be hidden from the ridge, but Grant didn't think whoever had been up there was up there still. And he didn't think they were gone.

"Okay," Dahlia agreed.

Grant turned to the dog. "Willie. Follow." The dog wagged his tail in recognition of the order.

Grant fought down all the bad feelings, all the doubts. It was dangerous. Chances were high it was a trap. But, no, they could hardly just walk away from a potential sighting of her sister.

Dahlia was sure, and he knew what being desperate could do to a person, but…he just believed her. Couldn't help himself. She was sure, and so he'd be sure with her. *For* her.

He started forward, gun drawn, Dahlia far too close at his heels. He fought off the memories of old wars long gone as they moved down the street, as close to cover as he could manage. When they reached the last building, he leaned against the outer wall before crossing in front of the broken window.

"Stay here," he whispered to Dahlia while making the hand signal for stay at Willie. He could tell Dahlia didn't *want* to stay, but he gave her a stern look. "I mean it."

She swallowed but then nodded. Willie stood at the ready right next to her, and Grant had to trust the dog would sound an alarm if something was about to happen to her while he searched the building.

Grant eased into the doorway, gun first, careful to attempt to find cover. But there was none to find, and worse.

It was definitely a trap.

DAHLIA STOOD WITH her back to the building, Willie panting in front of her. But it felt like he was protecting her, somehow. However a dog could.

And all she could do was stand here and think... Rose. She *had* seen her. She kept replaying the moment in her mind. It was the same sweater. Rose's blond hair. Even the way she'd moved from the window to the door had been *Rose*.

Alive.

Dahlia wanted to cry, but her heart was beating so hard against her chest, and the silence made fear freeze any tears.

Too quiet. Too...much. And Grant moving into that building, alone and off-kilter because *she* wanted him to. She wasn't certain he believed her about seeing Rose, but he knew she needed to know. He *cared* about her well-being, about what she wanted.

It was hard to fathom, but when she focused on that, some of the shaky terror settled. She looked around the abandoned town. To her eye, there was absolutely no sign of anyone. Willie sat at her feet, clearly on watch, but not growling or tensed and ready. Just watchful.

Grant disappeared fully inside, and there wasn't a sound. She wasn't sure how he moved that quietly, but he did. She held her breath.

But nothing happened. He didn't return. There were no sounds. Eventually she had to let out her breath even though she'd been hoping to hold it until he returned so she could hear everything that happened.

Willie began to growl, low in his throat. His tail didn't wag. It was straight up. Ears perked, everything about him was like a dog ready to attack, but he didn't leave her side.

Which felt worse somehow, because to her, it meant the danger had to be coming from inside the building. Grant had told her to stay put, but what if…

"Willie," she whispered. She tried to think of any of the commands she'd heard Grant and Cash and the others use on the dogs. There was stay and still and… "Free," she whispered. Cash had said that once when he'd been training a few dogs, and when he'd said free, they'd all relaxed and scattered.

Maybe Willie would know her "free" meant to go wherever he needed to go. God, she hoped so.

Willie immediately headed for the door Grant had disappeared into. But just as he reached the opening, Grant's sharp order pierced the air. "Willie. *Go.*"

The dog seemed as confused as Dahlia felt, because it hesitated there in the doorway.

"Come here, sweetheart," a feminine voice said from inside the building. Willie growled, but Dahlia couldn't heed the warning.

"Rose." She hurried for the opening and then stopped dead in her tracks. It was Rose. Right there. In the sweater Dahlia had given her. But Dahlia couldn't rush forward and envelop her sister in a hug. Cry in relief and joy.

Because Rose was pointing a gun at Grant's head.

"You're here," Rose said, smiling widely at Dahlia. But she didn't sound like herself. Or maybe it was just the gun pointed at Grant. "At last."

"Rose, what are you doing?"

Rose let out a long breath, but she didn't drop the gun. "I have been *waiting*. Just waiting and waiting." Her smile never faltered, but this was not…

It was Rose, but something was wrong. Very, very wrong. "Rose, are you okay?"

"I'm wonderful. I've found the truth, Dahlia. And now you can too." The smile dimmed a little as her eyes moved to Grant. Who stood stock still, stoic and silent.

Dahlia couldn't imagine what she was thinking, but she didn't like the way Rose was studying him at all.

"Can you put down the gun? He…he's my friend. Please, put down the gun."

Rose pressed her lips together. "He'd have to put his gun down first."

"I'm not pointing it at you," Grant replied. And it was true. The gun in his hand was pointed at the ground. "I don't want to hurt you."

Rose scoffed. "I'm the one with the gun pointed at your head. How could you hurt me?"

"Please, Rose." Dahlia took a halting step forward but stopped because Rose seemed to tighten her grip on the gun. "He helped me find you. Aren't you… Why do you have a gun? It's okay. We can go home now."

"Home? I'm never going home."

Dahlia sucked in a breath. This was all wrong, but she didn't know why. She wanted to cry. Rose was alive. Here and *alive*, and Dahlia wanted nothing else to matter.

But Rose needed to stop pointing that gun at Grant. "I don't understand."

"You haven't found the truth yet," Rose said, and it was almost like the sister she knew. The kind voice but just a *thread* of bossiness. Even though Dahlia was older, she'd always been more timid and introverted. Rose had been the bigger personality, so as they'd gotten older, Rose had taken to telling Dahlia what to do.

Why did everything in the past few weeks seem to come back to her never doing what she wanted? Never standing up for herself? Always bending to make someone else happy or at peace?

It made her angry, and this was definitely the wrong time to be angry since *guns* were being pointed at people she cared about. Dahlia couldn't really believe Rose would kill Grant. Both because Rose wasn't a killer and because Grant, even in the more submissive position, somehow... *seemed* in control.

"Grant, you could—"

He looked at her for the first time since she'd entered, and his eyes were flat and cold. "No."

Dahlia didn't know what to do with either of these people. "What if you *both* put your guns down?"

"No," they said in unison. Willie even growled like he was also saying no.

"What are you going to do? Just point guns at each other all day? This is ridiculous. Rose, you're safe now. We don't have to go home, but we can get you out of here and to help."

"Help? Dahlia, I've found truth. I've found peace, and once you join us, everything will be perfect. I promise. Come with me. Leave *him* behind."

"Rose." Dahlia couldn't understand what was happening. Rose was part of the cult? Brainwashed or...something?

"I have to take you back," Rose continued. "There's no other choice."

Dahlia could tell Grant wanted to speak, but he didn't. She supposed he understood like Dahlia did that Rose wasn't going to listen to either one of them, but Dahlia had the better chance of getting through.

"You're safe now, Rose."

"And so are you." Rose turned her oddly black gaze to Grant. "I'll let you go, for Dahlia, if you leave. Right now. Don't come back." She looked around him. "You can leave the dog. We'll take good care of him. Won't we, sweetheart?"

Willie still growled.

"His name's Willie," Dahlia managed. She didn't dare look at Grant. "Come here, Willie." She crouched a little and patted her legs, and Willie trotted over. She screwed up the courage to look at Grant.

He had not moved. Not for the door. Not away at all. His expression was impassive, but she saw the flash of emotions in his eyes. Anger and frustration. She tried to beg him with her eyes. *Just leave. I'll get through to her.*

He shook his head infinitesimally, and he was just so…set on something. Determined and honorable somehow. She wanted to reach out and soothe him or beg him or *something*. Because Rose was here, but she wasn't herself, and Dahlia just knew they had to save her somehow.

Grant turned his attention to Rose, everything

about him cooling into stoic blankness. But his words were fierce and made Dahlia's heart tremble. "I won't leave Dahlia here with you."

Chapter Seventeen

Grant knew Dahlia wanted him to, and maybe it would have been smart. To go get backup. But he knew someone else was out there. He also knew Dahlia's sister was on something—whether by choice or by force—she was under the influence of some kind of drug.

He couldn't, even for a moment, leave Dahlia alone with her.

They had different coloring, but when staring at both women, it was easy to see they were sisters. The same build, the same mouth, the same too-skinny frame, likely borne of the past year more than anything natural.

But Rose was still his enemy. Until Dahlia was safe.

"I won't leave, but I'll go with you," he said. It was hard. He was not a born actor, but for Dahlia, he'd try. "My maternal grandfather was an elder in the Order of Truth."

Rose looked at him suspiciously. He didn't dare look at Dahlia. He hadn't mentioned it, and he doubted very much Mary or Anna had brought it up. Even with Anna's fascination with the cult, no one was too proud to be the descendent of a Truth elder, especially in Sunrise. It was why his parents had never thought the cult was much of a joke, why his family had always been uncomfortable with Truth and Eugene Green.

His mother had done a lot to make up for being born into the Islay family. Everyone had told him, both before and after his parents' disappearance that it was good she'd married a Hudson—one of the good, upstanding families. That maybe, just maybe, she wasn't tainted by her relations.

But some had wondered, when both his mother and father had disappeared without a trace, if it had been that Islay blood catching up with them.

"My grandmother left the Order when my mom was a child," Grant went on. "And my mother didn't want us to be a part of it, but I've always thought…" Hell, what kind of nonsense was he supposed to spout to get closer? "The truth sounded more like home than the outside world."

Rose's eyes were narrowed as she stared him down. She didn't believe him. He didn't expect her to right away, but he could be patient.

Because he damn well wasn't letting Dahlia just *go* with the woman. Clearly, Rose wasn't well. And no wonder. She'd been a prisoner of the Truth, likely brainwashed and drugged, for a year.

And if she'd chosen it? Well, he'd cross that bridge with Dahlia when they came to it.

"No one escapes the Order alive," she replied.

"They did after the federal raid."

Rose's mouth firmed. "Put down the gun," she said.

"Grant." He wasn't sure what Dahlia wanted from him now, to lay it down or hold on to it. To stay or to go, but he'd made his decision. They'd get into that cult together and burn it down from the inside.

And he'd keep Dahlia safe. If he had to die to do it.

So, very carefully, he crouched and put his gun on the ground. He could hear Dahlia suck in a breath.

They were at Rose's mercy now.

"Can't you put yours down now?" Dahlia asked, and Grant could tell she was trying to be gentle, but nerves assaulted her.

Grant wasn't feeling too free and easy either. One purposeful pull of the trigger, or even a mistake, and he'd be dead.

"You could easily overpower me," Rose said to him.

Grant straightened and held his hands up in a gesture of surrender while also slowly and casually angling his body so the gun wasn't aimed quite so squarely at his head.

"I could, but I'm not going to. I don't hurt women." *Unlike your little cult*, he thought with some bitterness. Because the violence against women and sacrifice of women had been a *big* part of the cult's identity back in the sixties and seventies. They'd railed against the women's movement and had taken out every last frustration on women. It was the human sacrificing and the arms stockpiling that had brought the Feds in, but it had still created decades of trauma for the women involved.

Including his mother.

Grant took a careful breath. He couldn't afford to get angry.

Rose bit her lower lip, looking so much like Dahlia that sympathy waved through him against his will. Maybe he couldn't be angry, but he also couldn't be swayed by her just yet. It was dangerous.

But he also knew, because Sunrise made sure everyone knew, just what the Order of Truth could do to a person against their will. Particularly a woman. So, it was his job to keep her safe too.

"Rose."

Rose looked over at Dahlia. She frowned a little and brought her free hand to her head. "We need to find Samuel." She didn't lower her gun, but she moved it a pinch, so it didn't feel quite so much like a headshot was imminent.

"What happens when you take us to the cult?" Dahlia asked. One of her hands rested on Willie's head like he was the source of all her calm.

"Dahlia, you don't know how lucky you are." Rose took a step toward her, and Grant had to physically hold himself back from stepping between them. It didn't seem like Rose would hurt Dahlia just for the hell of it, but…

The cult would.

The gun wasn't pointed at Grant anymore as Rose approached Dahlia, but it didn't make him feel any more at ease. Rose stood in front of her sister, gun pointed at the ground.

"Once Samuel gets here, we'll take you to the Lord." Rose reached out and touched Dahlia's hair reverently. "You're the Chosen One."

"I don't… What if I don't want to be?" Dahlia asked. She hesitated, then reached up and took her sister's hand. She drew it away from her hair but then held on.

Rose's expression flickered. "You're *chosen*," she repeated. "The *one*. I thought I could be for a while." She tried to smile, but it faltered. She was also starting to twitch a little. Almost like whatever high she'd been on was starting to wear off.

Grant really wanted to get that gun out of her hand.

He took a step toward her, watching to see if

she'd pay attention, but she kept talking to Dahlia as he crept along.

"I can't remember..." Rose shook her head. "It doesn't matter. It's just important that you're here and chosen, so you will be. You'll ascend. You're so lucky."

None of that sounded *lucky*, and Grant would be damned if he let Dahlia be anything in this cult. He was *this* close to being able to get the gun out of Rose's hand when he heard someone's approach. Though it was clearly careful and quiet, Willie sensed it too, growling low in his throat without leaving Dahlia's side.

Grant took a step away from Rose, not sure what they'd be greeted with when whoever it was made an appearance. But he didn't want to look like he was a danger to anyone, and he'd rather position himself between the doorway and Dahlia so she wasn't a target.

She was *clearly* the target.

When the man finally appeared, almost as quiet as a ghost, Grant didn't bother to hide a scowl. "You."

One of the men from the road stood there, and when he recognized Grant, he smirked. He didn't have a gun and didn't reach for one, but a knife was holstered on his hip—much like the one that had stabbed Grant.

"You were only supposed to get the Chosen One, child."

All women in the cult were called child, regardless of age. Grant didn't know how anyone stomached it. But the shakes Rose was beginning to have explained something. She was definitely coming off some kind of drug.

And it didn't quite make sense to him, how a woman would be so elevated as to be chosen in this cult who had, as far as he knew, always treated women as second-class citizens.

"He's a descendent," Rose said.

This Samuel studied Rose, likely seeing the same things Grant did, regarding her shakes.

"Child, did you eat your breakfast this morning?"

"I was too excited to eat."

His frown deepened, then he turned to Grant. "What kind of descendent?"

Grant didn't want to tell him. He didn't want to be a part of this. He remembered, too clearly, how much any mention of the cult had bothered his mother.

But there was also Dahlia, too much a target of this horror. So he had to swallow his aversion and do whatever it took to save her. "Islay."

Samuel's eyes widened. "An *elder*? I don't believe you."

"Spirit Islay was my grandfather."

"That makes you the son of traitors."

Grant shrugged, and he fought for his next words to come out sounding as gross as they were. "I can't control what the women in my family did."

Samuel nodded thoughtfully. "You'll be tested, but we can use the numbers if you pass. Rose, search him."

Rose shuffled over to him. She took the phone and keys out of his pocket, then his wallet. She rifled through, took the cash and shoved it in a pocket of her dress.

She did not get the knife in his boot. Grant had a bad feeling he was going to need it.

"He's clear," she offered to Samuel.

Samuel nodded. "All right. Let's go before someone comes looking for them. Throw their things in their truck."

Rose scurried off to do just that. Grant watched Samuel. He could overpower the man, but he wasn't sure where it would lead them. And Rose still had her gun, so when she came back...

No, there were too many risks. Still, he inched closer to Dahlia and Willie. Once close enough, he took Dahlia's hand in his. Samuel was paying no mind to that, so Grant gave her hand a reassuring squeeze.

She leaned into him a little bit as they stood there faced with a man who was part of some cult that thought Dahlia was chosen for the color of her hair.

"It'll be all right," he murmured. One way or another, he'd make sure of it.

EVERYTHING WAS SO SURREAL, but Dahlia found holding Grant's hand gave her a certain amount of grounding. Maybe none of this made sense, and maybe her being chosen or not, they were clearly in a lot of danger, but they were in it together. And Grant had gotten her out of danger before.

Of course, he'd gotten stabbed in the process.

She glanced uneasily at the gun Rose still held in her hand when she reentered the store.

"Tie them together," the man named Samuel ordered Rose.

Rose moved to hand Samuel the gun but then seemed to think better of it and looked around for someplace to put it.

Dahlia exchanged a glance with Grant. For whatever reason, it seemed some people in their group wouldn't or maybe even couldn't touch guns. It was something to file away.

Rose took the cord Samuel handed her and moved over to Grant and Dahlia. She noted their joined hands with a little frown—not of disapproval exactly but of consideration. Rose looked up at Dahlia, but Dahlia couldn't read her sister's expression. When she'd always been able to.

Was it the year of no contact, of thinking she was dead? Or was it whatever this cult had done to Rose? Or worse, was it that Dahlia had never really known her sister at all?

Dahlia let out a shaky breath. There had to be some way to get through to Rose. But it likely wasn't going to be in front of the beady-eyed man standing in the doorway.

Rose wrapped the cord around Dahlia and Grant's wrists, allowing them to still hold hands. She shook as she tied, but the bonds were still strong, and allowed a bit of lead that she handed to Samuel.

So they were like dogs on a leash.

Samuel gave the lead a tug. "Follow along. The Lord will have to decide if you're telling the truth, Blood of Islay. Chosen One, there will be a grand celebration in your honor."

Dahlia couldn't find a way not to react to the words *Chosen One*. It made her shudder and feel sick to her stomach. She'd never wanted to be chosen by much of anyone, but she *really* didn't want to be chosen by monsters.

Samuel pulled the lead, and she and Grant were jerked forward. Out of the building and then down the middle of Main Street, as if they were being paraded through the town, except there was no one there to cheer.

Willie trailed after them. Rose had given him a little water back in the building, so Dahlia felt like he would at least be treated well. God, she hoped so.

She dared to look up at Grant in the fading sunlight. He appeared as stoic as ever, but she worried about his stab wound. She worried about everything he'd said back in the building.

Had he been telling the truth? Or was he trying to trick Rose? Dahlia had the sneaking suspicion everything he'd said had been true, and it was that truth that had made him dismissive and uncomfortable about every mention of Truth from the beginning until this moment.

It explained Anna's interest, Mary's concern. It explained *everything*.

He hadn't wanted to say any of it, but he had so he could stay with her. So he could keep her safe. He'd sacrificed those truths he didn't want to deal with for her.

So she had to find a way to keep him safe too.

They walked and walked, it seemed like in circles. Until the sun fell, the air cooled and she found herself shivering under a vast, amazing array of stars. When Dahlia braved a look at Rose, she was following along, hugging herself and looking sickly in the silvery moonlight.

Dahlia wanted to say something, reach out, *do* something, but Samuel kept dragging them along, and it was clear whether it was out of force or brainwashing or her own choice, Rose had aligned herself with a cult.

Desperate people do desperate things. She'd said that herself, without ever thinking her sister would be the desperate one.

They climbed hills that felt like mountains. Dahlia's mouth was dry as dust, and her head pounded. She'd kill for a drink of water. She looked over at Grant, but with night getting darker and darker with every passing moment, she could only make out the shadow of him in the moonlight.

She worried about his stab wound. She worried about what would happen when they got wherever they were being led. She worried about everything.

Finally, after what could have only been hours, she started to see flickers of firelight and smell the smoke on the cold air. She was trying desperately to keep her teeth from chattering, but the air got colder and colder.

They got closer and closer, until Dahlia could make out a camp. Lots of little very temporary looking tents set up in a kind of circle around a large RV. Over to the west, a large bonfire was crackling, and many men were sitting around it eating and chatting. To the east, a group of women stood around a kind of cauldron with a much smaller fire. It looked like they were eating as well and cleaning up the remnants of making a meal.

Dahlia's stomach rumbled. Odd to be hungry *now* when emotions had made her incapable of feeling hungry for so long.

But Rose was alive. Maybe Rose wasn't herself. Maybe she was in danger. But she was alive. There was hope.

Or so Dahlia thought. A lot of that hope began to fade when a man approached them. He was dressed in a white robe, and she knew at once he was the man from the security footage. Bald, but a carbon copy of a younger Eugene Green.

"Samuel. My child." He pressed his palms together in front of him, but even in the firelight, Dahlia could see his eyes lock on her. "You've brought me all I desire."

Chapter Eighteen

Grant called upon every last cell of control not to react. He wanted to fly forward and tackle the robed man to the ground. Stop him from ever laying eyes on Dahlia again.

But he didn't. Couldn't. Though some of the cult members clearly didn't carry guns, some did, and he had to find a way to get Dahlia and Rose out of this unharmed.

And bring *all* these people to justice.

The man's eyes turned to him, and his smile turned into a sneer. "Why have you brought *this*?"

"Lord of Truth, this man claims he's of the elder's blood," Samuel said reverently. He handed the lead on the rope to the other man. "Claims blood Islay."

"Islay? Islay are traitors."

"He says the women were traitors," Samuel replied, head bowed.

This leader, his *Lord of Truth*, nodded as if that made sense, just as Samuel had.

"My Lord," Samuel continued. "The child did not eat her breakfast this morning."

"This is a serious infraction, child," the man said to Rose.

"I'm sorry," Rose said, and her voice shook—part of it the comedown on whatever drug she clearly missed at breakfast and part fear. "I'll atone at once."

She was the main reason he was in this mess, but he couldn't stop the tide of sympathy. Clearly she'd gotten in over her head, even if she'd chosen the cult.

Except Dahlia was the Chosen One somehow. Whatever *that* meant. Even the man before them, this Lord of Truth, looked at her like all the answers in all the world existed in her.

Grant wanted that to be a reason to believe she'd be safe, that she'd have some power in the situation, but he knew too much, had seen too much. His own grandmother and mother had escaped this.

There was no safety in this cult for anyone, but especially for a woman.

As if to prove it, Samuel took Rose off deeper into the camp, and Grant couldn't be sure if it was to help her or hurt her. Dahlia watched her sister go with worry, and Grant could only squeeze Dahlia's hand, a silent promise they would figure this out.

Somehow.

"I will show you to your tent, Chosen One. Blood of Islay, we will have to convene a meeting to decide what to do with you. Come this way."

Before Grant even opened his mouth to protest, Dahlia was doing it for him.

"No," she said firmly, her grasp on his hand tightening even though their wrists were still tied together. "He has to stay with me."

"Chosen One—"

"If I am chosen and promised and all those other things your men shouted at me when they stopped us on the road a few weeks back, then you…you have to listen to me and do as I say… in this."

She faltered over only a few words. If Grant could have groaned without the man hearing him, he would have. This was hardly the best way to go about it. The man who fancied himself some kind of lord narrowed his eyes, and Grant began to open his mouth, yet again, to stand up for Dahlia. Defend her somehow.

But she did it herself before he could.

"You need me," she said firmly to the man. "You need me to be happy. Until the time."

Time… She seemed so sure, but Grant didn't have a clue what she was talking about.

"Perhaps, but we must test him. We cannot allow just anyone onto our sacred ground."

"You can if the Chosen One wills it."

The man's eyebrows raised. "You've studied us, Chosen One. I'm impressed."

Grant wished what he felt was impressed, but it was only dread and fear that they were getting deeper and deeper into something he couldn't control or escape from safely with Dahlia.

Not just her. Her and Rose, because he knew Dahlia wouldn't leave without her sister. He knew he couldn't ask her to. Rose was a victim here, even if she'd made some dubious choices in how she'd ended up in this mess.

"I presume you wish to share a tent then?"

"Yes," Dahlia said, chin angled upward. Almost regally. She reminded him a little of Mary when she was doling out orders, then figured that's who she was trying to emulate in the moment. If it had been any other situation, he might have smiled.

He'd once had to learn how to be tough too, or tough in a different way than he'd been used to. After his parents had left, he'd had to help Jack run the house. Be the ones the younger kids looked up to. He'd had to never show fury or impatience or any of those other emotions that had been roiling inside of him at sixteen.

So, he'd learned how to be the adult in the situation long before he'd been ready. He'd learned how to be a leader no matter how terrifying that had been.

It wasn't easy, but Dahlia had found some of

that leadership, that bravery, despite all the things tumbling around inside of her. He was proud of her.

"All right. Do you know when the time is, my Chosen One?" the Lord asked.

Dahlia swallowed, and though her expression appeared not to change, he felt her hand tremble in his. "No, not exactly."

The man smiled, sending a cold chill down Grant's spine. "Good. It's best when the anticipation is high."

"Pete," the man shouted and clapped his hand. Another skinny man scrambled over. He clearly had a gun tucked into the back of his pants. He didn't wear a robe, and Grant was beginning to think that meant something. The robed men didn't carry weapons. Maybe they were too holy?

"Show them to the Chosen One's tent. Keep them tied until they're inside."

Pete nodded. "Yes, my Lord." Then he was given the lead of the rope and pulled them farther into the center of the camp.

Behind the RV, a large tent was set up—much nicer and bigger than the others. It had its own little fire in front being tended by a woman who didn't look up as the man named Pete led them into the large tent.

He then silently untied the cords from their hands. He bowed to Dahlia, then left.

The tent had a large cot with many blankets,

lanterns and decorations. A cooler of food and drinks. Like…the glamping catalogs Mary had shown him one time that had made Jack's lip curl.

But this was a cult. It was beyond creepy. Beyond strange, and Grant knew…there was something he was missing. He turned to face Dahlia. *She* knew more than she wanted him to.

The flap of the tent closed, but Grant was under no illusion they were alone. It was just canvas, and the shadows outside were clear enough. There was a guard posted at the flap door—not robed, so he likely had access to a gun. There was the woman at the fire, who was definitely within hearing distance and was no doubt watching the tent.

"We should probably take turns sleeping," Dahlia offered into the quiet warmth of the tent. She was shivering now.

He couldn't stand it, so he wrapped his arms around her and pulled her close, though it caused a twinge where he'd been stitched up. She leaned into him, the tenseness of her shoulders slowly relaxing as she breathed carefully.

"Explain all this to me," he said, still holding her close.

Her shoulders tensed once again. "Grant…"

"No. No placating. No beating around the bush." He rubbed a hand up and down her back, hoping to warm her or stop her shaking. "Explain it to me. The Chosen One. The time."

She looked so pained, so twisted up, he wished he could comfort her. But he needed the truth first.

"They're going to sacrifice me."

DAHLIA HADN'T TOLD GRANT, or anyone, everything she'd learned in her research of the cult. Maybe she'd even denied it to herself a little bit, but here in the middle of all this…bizarre behavior, she knew it was true.

She would be sacrificed. There was a ritual though, one the cult had to follow to the letter. It hadn't been fully documented in the books, but enough that she knew she was safe until…well, until they decided she wasn't.

But by not telling anyone, she had gotten here. She had found out Rose was alive, and now they just had to save her. And themselves.

"Like hell they are," Grant said with more vehemence than she'd expected. His grip tightened, and she supposed she should feel scared by the threat of violence in his tone, but mostly she felt safe. Protected. Here in the shelter of his arms, she felt like they could really handle this.

But he pulled her away gently with enough of a pull that she had to look at him. Look at the anger and…*hurt* in his eyes.

"Is there anything else you've been keeping to yourself?"

"I didn't know…"

He raised his eyebrows, and the lie died in her throat. It wasn't fair to lie to him when all he'd ever done was try to help. "Yes, I read about the Chosen One and the ritual sacrifice. And, yes, I understood because of how they viewed women and blood...red hair that they might want me for that."

"And you didn't think to *mention* it?"

"I couldn't. I *couldn't*. I knew you'd try to lock me away in some safe room and handle it all yourself. If I had told you, I wouldn't know Rose was alive. We wouldn't be here with the opportunity to stop this. To get Rose *home*."

"Fine. You got what you want. Are you happy?"

It hurt. Because it wasn't just his usual straightforward demeanor. That was betrayal in his tone, lashing out to hurt *her*. But he didn't drop his hands from her shoulders. He didn't release her and step away, so she held on to that.

"No," she said, working to swallow down the tears that threatened. "None of this makes me happy, Grant."

He closed his eyes as if in pain. "I'm sorry," he murmured, then pulled her close again. "Damn it, Dahlia. I *would* have locked you away. This is too dangerous. It's too much of a risk." He blew out a breath that ruffled her hair. She rubbed her palms up and down his back, both assurance and...well, it was a very nice back.

"You really don't know how long it'll be?" he asked, still holding her to him.

"No, that was one of the details that was pretty vague. Only the Lord of Truth knows, I think. Or decides? But they have to keep me happy until that time. Maybe I could ask them to let Rose go?"

He pulled her back again, and this time his hands moved up her shoulders to frame her face. "Dahlia, she'd have to want to go."

Dahlia closed her eyes against the stab of pain the truth caused. "I know. But…maybe if they told her she could. Maybe she's just afraid. Maybe…"

"She's being drugged," Grant said. "The whole breakfast thing… Too weird to just be breakfast."

"Do you think they're all drugged?"

"It's possible. There was nothing about that in the books you read?"

"No, but they don't speak of the women usually. They're just the servants, more or less, for the men and the truth. The only exception is the Greens, or in this case, the Green bloodline. And only if you're born with red hair." Dahlia didn't know how to feel about that. How Rose must feel about it, drugged or not. A twist of fate, and their situations could be reversed.

"We should get some rest," Grant said, lowering his voice to a whisper, bringing his mouth close to her ear. "They'll have us watched at night. But tomorrow morning, you could say you want a tour. I'll be by your side. We'll figure out where Rose is and map a route out of here."

She had to swallow to focus on the words and not the sensations of his big calloused hands on her face, his breath against her ear. "Do you know where we are?" she asked, attempting her own whisper.

It wasn't about sensations. It was about anyone out there not hearing them.

"I have a general idea. The good news is that even if they covered our tracks, my family isn't going to let us disappear into thin air. They know what we were looking into. They have Kory Smithfield. Anna had some leads."

Dahlia nodded. "You get up earlier than I do. You're injured. You should sleep first."

He frowned at this, but she wasn't about to give up. "They'll likely come wake us up at dawn. Would you rather be the one awake and watching then or the one asleep?"

His frown turned to a scowl.

"It's practical," she insisted, because it *was*. And because if she laid down now, she wouldn't sleep. She'd think about what it felt like in his arms. She'd think about Rose drugged. She'd think about being sacrificed.

That was *quite* the warped combo.

"Can I trust you to wake me up in an hour or two?"

"Of course."

He raised an eyebrow, a clear sign the *of course* was over the top. Which was fair. But she wanted him to truly rest, so she lifted her hand and fitted it over his cheek. "I promise to wake you up. I know I have kept things from you at times, but I don't make promises I don't plan to keep."

He sighed. "It's the 'plan to' that worries me."

She leaned up and gave him a quick friendly peck on the lips. "Good night, Grant."

He grunted, and after a few moments of holding her in place and studying her, he let go and went and lay down on the cot. He fell asleep quickly, and Dahlia set to looking around the tent for something she could use to rebandage his side tomorrow.

She could, of course, demand first aid from one of the cult members, but she wasn't sure she trusted them—not to help him, not to bring suitable bandages.

When that didn't yield anything, she studied the food options, then thought about Rose's discussion about breakfast.

No, she couldn't trust the food or water either.

A noise had her turning to look at Grant. He was asleep—eyes closed, chest rising and falling, but he muttered something, then turned his head violently to one side as if in pain. She took a step forward as he began to thrash. The groan of pain startled her so much she jumped.

But then she hurried to his side. "Grant. Grant. You're having a dream." Wasn't there something about not waking people up? Or was that sleepwalking? She didn't know. She knew he wouldn't want her to see him like this, but worse, he wouldn't want anyone outside to hear him moaning and muttering.

She nudged his shoulder. "Grant, wake up. It's okay. You're…" Well, he wasn't okay, was he? He was the prisoner of a cult.

He grabbed her suddenly. She bit back a scream, because he simply maneuvered her behind him, like he was shielding her from something. "Stay down," he ordered, but she was pretty sure he was still asleep. Or trapped in some kind of dream anyway.

Dahlia didn't know what to do but wrap her arms around him from where she was wedged behind him and the cot's frame. She pressed her cheek to his back. "Grant, it's okay. Wake up. I'm right here."

Something changed. His breathing was ragged, but she could tell he'd woken up. He kept himself tense. There was no more muttering, ordering or thrashing. He held himself still—too still.

"I'm…sorry," he said, sounding ragged and, worse, mortified.

"Don't be sorry." She stayed exactly where she was. Hugging him, cheek pressed to his back. "You have… PTSD?"

"No. Not like... I have dreams sometimes. Flashbacks. But they deemed me A-OK and all that. It's just...normal, I guess."

"Of course it is." She hugged him tighter. "You saw terrible things. That doesn't just leave you."

He sucked in a breath and let it slowly out. "Did I hurt you?"

"Don't be silly," she said. "You tried to protect me."

He nodded. "Yeah, doing a real bang-up job," he muttered. But she could tell he was trying to deflect from the dream.

"Grant. What did you dream about?"

He stiffened in her arms and tried to move, but she held tight. Eventually, he put his hand over hers locked at his chest.

"My superior officer was shot. I tried to get him out under heavy fire. Not regulation, but I did it. Or almost. He had a wife and two kids at home. I had no one. But he died, and I survived."

It broke her heart to hear him say it, to know he'd felt it. When she'd seen him with his family. "You had brothers and sisters and a niece who need you very badly."

"You don't understand, Dahlia." This time he pulled her hands off him. He didn't get off the cot like she expected him to though. He turned to face her. Serious. Tired. "They did just fine without me."

"You underestimate yourself. The Hudson machine does not work if you're not one of the cogs in it."

He almost smiled. "Cogs, huh?"

"It's true. You're a unit. You don't function without each other. I'm sure it comes from losing your parents, but I bet if you asked your siblings—any one of them, even Jack—how things ran without you, they'd say not as smoothly, as balanced as *with* you. You're the counterweight. Without you, Jack's too hard, and Cash is too isolated, and Palmer is too—" she struggled for a word "—wild, I suppose. Same with Anna."

"What about Mary?"

Dahlia considered. "Well, probably too internal." She could relate.

"I don't know about all that."

"I think you do. I think you needed it pointed out to you, but I think now that you see it, you can't unsee it." She studied his face and knew it was true. But she also knew… "You haven't told them, have you?"

"I'm sure they know I've had a nightmare or two."

"But you don't talk to anyone about it."

"I just talked to you."

She didn't know much about PTSD. She knew Grant though. Somehow, she understood him. In these few weeks of watching him—with his family, with the dogs, with her. She knew who he was.

She reached out for him, putting her hands on his cheeks, making sure he had to look her in the eye. "It's your turn to promise me something."

"What?" he replied, clearly trying for unmoved, stoic and failing.

"Just talk to someone. It can be a sibling, a friend. It could probably even be a dog."

He was silent for a long stretch of moments. "What about you?"

Her heart melted. Right here in the middle of this mess she just…fell for him. Hook, line and sinker. "It could always be me."

After another long silence, he nodded. Then he got up off the cot and gestured to it. "It's your turn to get some sleep, Dahlia. Dawn will come soon enough."

Since he was right, and they had a cult to outmaneuver tomorrow, she nodded and did as she was told. After all, she knew Grant, and a nod from him was as good as a promise. And he was not a man who went back on promises.

So, she laid down and slept. And when she dreamed, she only dreamed of sunshine and him.

Chapter Nineteen

Grant could let the embarrassment eat him alive, or he could focus on the task at hand. He couldn't do any recon in this tent, but leaving Dahlia sleeping and vulnerable was out of the question.

He looked at his stitches. He'd popped one or two, but they'd stopped bleeding and had scabbed over. He couldn't find anything sterile to use as a bandage, so he'd just have to hope he'd done enough and they'd be out of this soon enough that it wouldn't matter.

His family hadn't known where he and Dahlia had been going, and that's what a person got for sneaking and lying, he supposed. But still, Grant had no doubt they'd started a search by dinnertime, and they'd know to look into Truth. Then, once they found his truck with all his and Dahlia's things in it, they'd be able to track them here.

It would take time though, especially over the dark nighttime hours. They were well and truly out in the middle of nowhere at this camp. Oh, the Samuel guy had tried to trick him with the circles and endless walking up and down hills, but Grant knew this stretch of Wyoming better than anyone, aside from his own family. He might not know the exact map pinpoint, but he knew well enough where they were and how to head back to civilization.

What he didn't know was how to convince Rose to come with them. He could outsmart a cult. Between what he knew and what Dahlia knew, and his own skills, Grant had no doubt he could get out of here.

But Dahlia wouldn't leave her sister, so Grant couldn't either.

Grant looked at Dahlia curled up on the cot. She slept peacefully, which was a relief. They'd need their strength and their wits about them. He hated that she was here surrounded by these people who wanted to *sacrifice* her, but they had a bit of a reprieve tonight.

Maybe if she could convince her sister not to eat the breakfast they were so intent on tomorrow, they could convince her to leave once backup showed up.

The problem was, even drugged, Rose shouldn't be okay with Dahlia being *sacrificed*. Even brainwashed, the idea of her sister being killed should be reason enough not to have brought Dahlia here.

Grant didn't like it, but of course he didn't like

any of this. So he had to find a way to get them both out of here before any rituals started.

He heard the shuffle of people outside, saw shadows moving, and then the tent opened. Grant didn't pretend not to be awake and watching. He hoped they got the message that he'd protect Dahlia at all costs.

"Good morning," the man who'd brought them here last night boomed, making Dahlia jerk awake and sit up in the cot wide-eyed.

Grant scowled. "Thanks for the wake-up call, Pete."

Pete bowed at the waist. Hell, this place was weird as could be. "You are most welcome, Blood of Islay."

Grant exchanged a look with Dahlia. She was frowning like he was, but she looked sleep tousled and still a little out of it.

"Come. It's time for breakfast, Chosen One."

Dahlia rubbed her eyes then got off the cot. "It's a bit early to eat, isn't it?"

"We eat with the sun. We worship a new day and the opportunity to find truth in the lies." He led them out of the tent. The fire from last night had died, and there didn't seem to be anyone around tending it anymore.

"Where's Willie? Where's my dog?" Dahlia asked, looking around as they walked.

"The children are taking very good care of him."

Dahlia exchanged a glance with Grant. Worry and confusion. Grant could only shrug his shoulders. They hadn't seemed intent on hurting the dog, so he had to hope that might work in their favor.

Pete led them past the RV and smaller tents to a long table. The women all sat at it with the men standing around. There were bowls in front of each woman with some kind of oatmeal mixture. Rose sat at the end of one bench, and Willie was on the ground next to her. His tail began to wag when he saw Dahlia.

"This is your seat, Chosen One," Pete said, pointing to a chair at the head of the table next to Rose.

All the women bowed and murmured chants of "Chosen One." Grant had to fight the urge to pick her up and walk her right the hell out of here—sister and any objections be damned.

But she wanted her sister, and he wanted to take these people down. So he stood where he was and bit his tongue.

"Blood of Islay." He was handed a stick of some kind of jerky. "Your breakfast, brother." Grant studied the jerky, then the women and the men.

He didn't know if it was more or less disturbing the men clearly weren't drugged since it appeared all the women were.

The men all stood around the women, watching as if to make sure every last drop was eaten. Grant wondered if this was an everyday occurrence or if it was happening today because Rose had skipped her meal yesterday, so there were extra precautions in place. He glanced at the man next to him, who'd handed him the jerky.

"Do we always eat standing up?" he asked, attempting to be casual.

The man looked around. "We must protect our children."

Grant tried not to make a face at that. It was just so disturbing. Not one of these women appeared to be under eighteen. He supposed the only saving grace was he hadn't seen any evidence of *actual* children.

The man—the "Lord"—from yesterday stepped forward, taking a place at the opposite end of the table Dahlia sat at. He looked at the women and their bowls of oatmeal. "Children, I am your Lord of Truth. And here, in each bowl, is the truth. Eat so that you too may see a glimmer of the truth I feed you."

Dahlia looked over her shoulder at him, eyes wide, clearly worried that she was going to eat.

Over his dead body.

So, Grant would have to create a diversion.

DAHLIA TRIED NOT to panic, but she was not going to eat this laced oatmeal. She looked back at

Grant, who stood there looking stoic somehow. But she knew he wasn't.

She wished she had his ability to turn off panic or anger or whatever feeling he was hiding, but she felt like every emotion chased across her face. Refusal and fear and panic.

Grant gave her a little nod, not a *go ahead* nod, she knew. But more something like *I'll take care of it*.

The Lord of Truth blathered on about the importance of eating every bite, of all the truth you could find with a clean bowl.

It was *insanity*. Dahlia tried not to get hung up on how anyone could fall for this nonsense. *Desperate people do desperate things*.

Had Rose been desperate? Had all these women?

Willie barked, causing Dahlia to jerk in surprise. The sudden movement upended her bowl, but before anyone could move to do anything about it, Willie hopped up next to her *on* the table. Then he began to run up and down it, yipping happily while women jumped up in an effort to grab their bowls or stop the dog.

But he ran, bounced, barked. He didn't growl. He acted like he was playing some kind of entertaining game, and every woman's shriek and every man's order to stop was only part of the game.

Dahlia looked at Grant. He was focused on

the dog and made a little noise, almost a whistle and a hand motion. Then Willie dismounted the table, barked like crazy and ran away from camp.

Some of the men took off after the dog. Some of the men were ordering the women to clean up or eat what had spilled. In the chaos, Dahlia leaned over to her sister.

"There are drugs in there," Dahlia said, feeling a little desperate to shake some sense into Rose. "You should avoid eating it at all costs."

"It helps," Rose said. "It is for our own good. It's the truth."

"No, it's for theirs." Dahlia looked around the table. "Try to remember what you felt like before you came here," Dahlia said—not just to her sister but to all of them who could hear her desperate whisper. Maybe they'd grown up in this horror, but maybe they were like Rose and had been kidnapped into it.

Even if Rose had somehow come to believe in it—which Dahlia found hard to accept of her vibrant, passionate sister—Rose wouldn't have joined this cult without a word, leaving everyone behind to worry about her. Dahlia couldn't believe that.

"Avoid what they give you. Just for a day or two. See how you feel. I promise you. It might be bad at first, but you'll be clearer. You'll find the *real* truth. Not their truth."

"Blasphemy," a woman hissed.

But Dahlia ignored her. She kept her gaze on Rose. Imploring. "Please. Just avoid it as best you can. Let your mind clear."

Rose held her gaze, almost like she was considering what her sister was telling her. Then she smiled, but it was a creepy smile, like the Lord of Truth. "Dahlia, you should try our way. The real truth. It's…transcendent."

Dahlia swallowed, hating what she was about to say, but if she had to play the Order of Truth's game to get her sister out of here, then so be it. "I'm the Chosen One, Rose. Wouldn't I know best?"

Rose blinked at that, then looked down at her spilled oatmeal. When she looked back up at Dahlia, it was with an expression Dahlia remembered from their childhood: stubborn rebellion. She took her spoon and began to scoop up every spilled drop of oatmeal. From the table to her mouth, defiantly eating every last bit.

Dahlia was speechless. She was literally rendered immobile by her sister's behavior.

But then Rose ate Dahlia's too. Dahlia wanted to believe it was some kind of self-sacrifice. She was desperate to believe it. But Rose looked at her defiantly as if to say, *See, I'm right. You're wrong.*

"Rose," Dahlia said, wanting to cry. "Why?"

"You don't understand. You can't understand." She was starting to look angry. Certainly not scared or even relieved Dahlia was here. She just looked *mad*. "You're the Chosen One and you don't even understand," Rose said, sounding a bit like a petulant child.

"I understand. Being chosen means they're going to *kill* me," Dahlia replied in a whisper. Most of the men were making sure the women ate their oatmeal off the table or had gone off to find the dog, but they could start paying attention to *her* at any minute.

"Yes," Rose said. As if it were a good thing. A *right* thing. That they wanted her dead eventually in some ritual sacrifice.

Dahlia could only gape at Rose, who smiled.

"And aren't you lucky?"

Chapter Twenty

Once the breakfast ruckus died down and was cleaned up, Grant and Dahlia were escorted back to their tent. Grant was relieved. Standing around the group of people was just…too much. The thought of his mother growing up in this nightmare was painful and the threat of Dahlia being *sacrificed* too much to bear.

There were murmurs about hunting down the dog, but Grant was convinced Willie had gotten a good enough head start. Willie would go find Cash or someone and lead them back.

He would have sent him last night if he'd gotten the chance, but this was perfect. It had allowed Dahlia to avoid eating the drugged oatmeal. Grant didn't know what diversion he'd manage for lunch, but they'd cross that bridge when they came to it.

Before Pete left them, Dahlia spoke. "I want to see my sister. In here. Alone."

Pete blinked, looked at Grant almost like he was looking for permission, then back at Dahlia. "I don't know…"

"I want to see my sister. Do as you're told by the Chosen One, or ask your Lord of Truth. I don't care, but I want her brought to me. Here."

Grant had never heard her speak so forcefully. What happened at breakfast was clearly bothering her, and he wanted to comfort her in some way, but he didn't know how. This was a mess of a situation.

Pete scuttled out of the tent, and Grant figured it would be a while before he returned. He didn't seem very…confident. He'd likely go talk to the lord guy first.

Dahlia was pacing, eyebrows furrowed, tension and upset radiating from her. He couldn't let her keep stewing, so he stood in her path. When she stopped abruptly and looked up at him, he held his arms to the sides.

She closed her eyes, her expression crumpling, and she fell into him. He wrapped his arms around her and held her close. She took a deep breath, and her shoulders relaxed. "Grant, she ate both of our bowls," Dahlia said, voice scratchy.

"She was saving you." He wasn't sure it was true, but he hoped it was for Dahlia's sake.

But she shook her head. "I wish I believed that were true." She looked up at him without releasing her grip or making him release his hold on her. A few tears had fallen over. "She wasn't saving me or doing anything selfless. At least, she didn't act like she was. It was like she was…defying me because I told her they were drugged. Or trying to prove something, like she wants to be here? I don't know, but she thinks I'm *lucky* for being the sacrifice. Grant, I'm afraid I just can't reach her."

Grant brushed some of Dahlia's hair out of her face. "We'll keep trying," he promised.

She let her forehead rest against his chest as she took another ragged breath. "I can't leave this place without her."

"I know." He rubbed her back and then…told her something he swore he'd never tell anyone. "My mother once, and only once, told us about escaping the Order. How hard it was, how many tries it took. How many times her mother would be on the verge of giving up. The only thing that kept my grandmother going was not wanting this life for her daughter."

Dahlia looked up at him. Her eyes had filled again, in sympathy as much as worry over her own sister. So he made her a vow he wouldn't break. "We'll keep trying until we get her out. I promise you that."

A few more tears fell, but she didn't sob or cry. She just squeezed her eyes shut, and the tears fell over. "I don't know how I'll ever repay—"

He took her by the chin. "Dahlia. Stop thinking of this as an exchange. I'm here not just because you hired me—in fact, if that was why, we never would have been taken by that Samuel guy. We wouldn't have been in Truth. We'd have listened to Jack and turned it all over to law enforcement weeks ago. I'm here because I care about you."

She opened her eyes. Met his gaze. For a moment, she simply looked at him. When she spoke, it was with the kind of gravity that humbled him. "I care about you too, Grant."

But anything else they might have said or done was interrupted by the flap being lifted and Rose entering the tent.

She studied them standing in each other's arms. Even with tears on Dahlia's face, there was something cool in Rose's expression that Grant didn't trust. So he didn't let Dahlia go. Didn't step away. He wanted to…protect her somehow.

Because Dahlia was probably right, and there was no reaching Rose—at least here, drugged and in the cult. Dahlia knew her sister, and Grant knew how this cult in particular could mess with a person and warp them.

But he also knew Dahlia would never just let Rose stay here, whether Rose wanted to leave or not. Dahlia hadn't given up on Rose when she thought she was dead. Why would she give up on her sister alive and standing right here?

Besides, Grant had vowed to get her out, so he'd find a way.

DAHLIA FELT… God, she was so tired of thinking about how she felt. The swings of emotion were such a pendulum, and in the midst of it all, she was in this strange place, and her sister…was a stranger.

"You wanted to see me?" Rose said. She sounded sweet and happy, but there was something about the way she looked at Grant that made Dahlia uncomfortable.

"I wanted to make sure you were okay. Since you ate my meal this morning, you must have ingested twice the amount of drugs meant for any one person."

Rose smiled wide, but her pupils were so dilated her eyes were nearly black. "It was oatmeal, Dahlia. Sustenance. The great gift of truth from the great Lord of Truth. You only have to accept his truth to be free."

Dahlia wanted to press her face into Grant's chest again and just…push all this fanatical talk away. She'd been prepared to deal with Rose being dead. Or even kidnapped. But somehow, being *part* of this cult, saying these things and seeming to believe them…

Dahlia just didn't know what to *do*. How did you get through to someone drugged and brainwashed?

But much like the past thirteen months, she knew she couldn't give up. "Rose, can you tell me how you ended up here?"

"The truth brought me," she said, still smiling.

"I think Dahlia meant something a little bit

more concrete," Grant offered. "You disappeared in Texas."

"No, I found the Lord of Truth in Texas," Rose corrected. Dahlia wouldn't call the look she sent Grant *mean* exactly, but it wasn't nice. "We didn't know you were the Chosen One then."

"How did you find that out?" Grant asked, earning another pointed look from Rose.

"Does it matter?"

"It does to me," Dahlia said earnestly.

Rose sighed heavily. She stood in one place, but her eyes darted around, and she occasionally shook a hand this way or that, like she was filled with an energy she couldn't quite control or decide what to do with.

"The Lord didn't like that you were looking for me, of course. I told him no one would care if I disappeared, and you proved me wrong, sister." It was accusation more than anything good. Like Dahlia *should* have forgotten her sister, assumed she was dead and moved on.

"I had to find out what happened to you," Dahlia replied, trying to keep the hurt out of her voice. Rose wasn't herself. She was *drugged*. Dahlia couldn't take anything at face value or be hurt by Rose's words. "How could I let it go? You *disappeared* into thin air. I thought I was searching for your murderer, Rose." She swallowed down the frustration, reminding herself Rose was alive, and that was what was impor-

tant. "I'll never give up on bringing you home."
It was a promise Dahlia had to keep.

Rose shook her head vehemently. "*This* is my
home. The Order is my home. I have a place here.
A role. Not like *home*. Constantly arguing with
our small-minded, simpleton parents."

"Rose…" Dahlia didn't have the words. She
knew her parents and Rose had a strained relationship, but this felt bigger. Here in the midst of
all this insanity.

"People care about me and for me here," Rose
continued. "The Lord took special care of me.
I'm a Green. I'm special."

"We *aren't* Greens."

"We are! We have the blood!" She stamped
her foot like a child, though Rose's temper had
always retreated to childishness if given the
chance. "And I was important until *you* came
along." Her fingers curled into fists. "I had to
bring you. The Lord saw you and then wanted
you. But you should have stayed in Minnesota.
You should have forgotten about me, and then
maybe *I* would have been chosen."

Dahlia didn't know how to comprehend this.
Being chosen meant being sacrificed. Being spe-
cial meant ending up *dead* in the Order of Truth.
Well, if you were a woman.

Why couldn't Rose see that?

Dahlia looked helplessly at Grant. His expression was one of sympathy. He understood what

this group could do to a person's mind, and he didn't judge.

But he also didn't know how to fix it. Change it. Did anyone?

"Don't I mean anything to you, Rose?" Dahlia asked, trying to keep her voice from shaking. "You're my sister. I love you."

"You're the Chosen One," Rose replied, her smile wild again. Her eyes darting everywhere. "This is the truth. You will meet the Lord in the sky. You will be free. And your ashes will lead us to a deeper truth." Rose moved forward with every word, reaching out much like the men had done by the highway.

But there was something far more menacing in Rose's eyes. Like she might reach out and try to choke the life out of Dahlia.

Grant stepped forward, blocking Dahlia and stopping Rose's forward progress.

Dahlia was shaken to her core. Her sister... wanted her dead.

Your sister who's been traumatized, drugged and brainwashed for a year. She tried to repeat that to herself over and over again, but she still felt dumbstruck, scared, betrayed.

"You could let us escape," Grant said to Rose. "Dahlia could disappear. Then you could be important again."

Dahlia tried to protest. How could he... How could Grant, of all people... How could he think she'd leave Rose here when he'd promised to help? Surely Grant understood that even with the threats, the anger, Dahlia would never leave without her sister.

Outside of the Order, she could find Rose help. She could have her *actual* sister back. She was sure of it. She had to believe it, hold on to that possibility. Just like no matter how hard she'd tried, she'd always held on to the possibility that Rose was alive.

And Rose *was* alive. There had to be a positive ending to this mess.

Rose seemed to consider Grant's proposition, and when Dahlia opened her mouth to find the air to argue, Grant gave her a firm shake of the head.

"Grant—"

He shook his head again. "I made a promise," he said softly. "I intend to keep it."

He'd promised to get Rose out of here. So… this was some sort of trick or plot or something, and she had to go along with it.

"I also made a promise," Rose said loftily. "To bring my Lord the Chosen One. To find the truth through your glorious sacrifice, Dahlia." Rose smiled once more.

Dahlia didn't know how to reconcile the fact that Rose looked almost exactly the same as she had the last time Dahlia had seen her, but there was…nothing on the inside that was the same.

In the silence that followed, Dahlia heard the

faint yip of a dog. Willie? Oh, she hoped not. Even though everyone had been kind to the dog, she had a bad feeling this morning's breakfast shenanigans would earn him some kind of punishment.

"Grant?"

His expression was unreadable. But she knew he'd heard it too. Still, he turned to Rose. "Think about letting us go. Or coming with us when we leave."

"You won't be going anywhere, friends," Rose said sweetly. "Except to the Lord in the sky." She wafted out of the tent.

Dahlia collapsed onto the cot. Her legs couldn't keep her up any longer. She buried her face in her hands, trying to think. She only looked up when she felt Grant's hand on her knee.

He was crouched in front of her at eye level, clearly worried. But before she could say anything, he spoke in a low whisper. "Help is here."

"What?"

"That bark? Willie's alerting. Cash or Palmer or *someone* from my family is here, Dahlia. We have to get out. Now."

Before Dahlia could protest or explain that despite everything, she couldn't leave without her sister, she heard people shouting. Grant ran for the tent flap, so she followed.

When they got out, people were running in the opposite direction. No one was paying much attention to them. But Dahlia heard Willie again. From behind.

She turned with Grant, and there across the open field was Willie. Just standing there. He let out another little yip, and Dahlia saw a flash of light.

Grant grabbed her. "Did you see that light?"

"Yes."

"It's Anna. Run for her. Right now. Don't stop. Don't look back. Just run to right where you saw her, no matter what you hear, no matter what happens. You run."

Her fingers curled into his sweatshirt. "What are you going to do?" she demanded, her heart beating overtime. He wasn't going with her, and she couldn't leave Rose *or* him.

He pried her fingers out of the fabric of his shirt. "I'm going to bring you your sister."

Chapter Twenty-One

Grant ran. He didn't have a gun, but he had the knife in his boot. The biggest challenge he faced was the fact he didn't know where Rose would be. Most of the people running around were too busy shouting orders or following them to pay him much mind.

He hoped it would stay that way. The men were all congregating around a kind of hole in the ground. Grant still ran, but when he looked back at the men, he realized what they were doing.

Pulling guns out of some sort of underground stockpile. *Hell.*

It didn't bode well for him, but he had to find Rose. He went around all the tents, even circled back and searched the RV, but he could not find any of the women, and the longer that went on, the more concerned he became.

He decided to return to where the men had been pulling weapons out of the ground in hopes they'd lead him to the women, but now they were gone too.

Damn cults.

He stilled and listened. Even though it was eerily quiet, at some point, he'd have to hear something to go on.

Old flashbacks threatened. Sand and blood and Sergeant Lincoln. Shouting and gunshots and explosions.

But he kept his eyes focused on the here and now. The grass beneath his feet. The sound of the tents flapping gently in the wind. In his mind, he retraced their path here yesterday. Up and down a few hills he'd thought were meant to distract, but maybe…

He headed east, the way they'd come. As he closed in on a hill, he heard it. The faint murmurs of people. So he climbed the hill carefully and silently.

Once close enough to the rise to peek over, he saw all of them in the distance, the men and women, but…the whole scene made his blood chill.

The women were all on their knees, men lined up behind them. With guns. There was another line of men behind them, all in robes that billowed in the wind. They didn't hold guns or any weapons.

They all faced north, and Grant realized even though he couldn't see them, law enforcement was somewhere over the second rise.

Anna had come in from the south in order to

get him and Dahlia out before law enforcement moved forward.

It was too much like that federal raid. Hostages. Stockpiles of arms and insanity. Too many people were going to end up hurt or even dead, and still…as he searched the faces of the women on their knees, he didn't see Rose.

Where the hell was she? Had she escaped?

He wished he could believe that, but after everything that had happened in their tent earlier, he couldn't.

If law enforcement was over that hill, these people were set up like the first wave to stop them. The first sacrifice. But there would be a second.

If Dahlia was still here, they'd want her.

Had they gone after her?

His heart felt as though it fully stopped at the idea. But he couldn't let that stop *him*. He turned and moved down the hill, focusing on silence. On stealth.

Not on the panic-inducing thought someone might have gotten to Dahlia and his sister.

But as he moved back through the camp, he heard lowered voices and had to slow. Had to use the tents as cover to creep closer and closer. Until he was at the place where the bonfire yesterday had been—a big stone circle.

But there was no fire lit today. At least yet. Because in the center of the stones was a big wooden pole. And the so-called Lord of Truth was tying Rose to it.

But the thing that made him fully stop in his tracks was the sheer volume of explosives littered around the both of them.

Hell.

As if sensing him, the Lord of Truth stopped and looked around. Grant was hidden by a tent, but as he studied the area, he realized it was just the three of them, and while the lord guy had explosives, he didn't seem to have a gun on him. The Lord was in robes. He was too holy to carry a gun.

Grant hoped.

So Grant did the only thing he could since his end goal was to get Rose out of this. For Dahlia. He pulled the knife out of his boot and stepped forward.

The man tightened the knot he was tying around Rose and the pole but glared at Grant. "I don't know what you think you're going to stop. Violence isn't the answer."

"Says the man tying a woman to a pole surrounded by explosives."

"A sacrifice is good and right. It will bring us the truth, the balance. And a way forward until we are once again reunited with the Chosen One."

"You'll never get your hands on her."

The man shook his head and stepped away from Rose. But that didn't make Grant feel any better, because he didn't think it would take much to set those explosives off. Enough explosives to take all three of them out.

"You brought this evil on us, Blood of Islay."

"Yeah, me. So let Rose…let the child go."

There was a moment in which the man seemed to actually consider it, and Grant used that moment of consideration to inch closer and closer.

The man's gaze turned to the explosives. To Rose. "She's not the Chosen One."

"No, she isn't," Grant agreed. Another step. One or two more, and he could tackle the guy without using the knife. "You should let her go."

"But sacrifice brings truth. We need truth to survive. You've brought the outside world upon us, Blood of Islay, and—"

Grant lunged. The man was so impressed with his own little speech that he didn't seem to see it coming. But he still fought like hell even once Grant got him to the ground.

But he wasn't an adept fighter. His attempts at punches were flailing and weak, the robe tangling his arms so that he couldn't get a good punch in. Grant had him pinned to the ground immobile in less than a minute. All the while, the man kept screaming about truth and sacrifice.

"I built this from the ashes! I am the original Lord's descendent. The true leader. I am the truth! There was nothing, and then I breathed the flame of truth back into it all!"

"You should have let it die." Grant pulled his fist back and focused on a spot that would ideally knock the man out for the time being. He used his full force for the blow, and the man went limp.

Grant blew out a relieved breath, but when he looked over at Rose, he swore and jumped into action.

DAHLIA HAD MADE it to Anna with Willie leading the way, and now they huddled behind a hill and waited.

Just waited.

It was driving Dahlia insane.

"How can you let him just…be out there risking his life?" she finally demanded when Anna looked as if she were having a grand old time relaxing.

Anna looked over at her and uncharacteristically seemed to consider her words. "Do you think Grant would just…be cool with us running in to help?"

Dahlia didn't say anything. She couldn't, because of course not.

"And given the choice, would he want to send someone else into all that in his place?"

Again, Dahlia didn't answer. It was pointless. She didn't know why she was arguing, she just… "I can't stand waiting around feeling purposeless."

"I get it. Trust me, more than you could ever

understand. But we rush in there, we mess up the plan and what they're doing. So we have to be careful and bide our time." Anna studied her for a long perceptive moment. "Grant's my brother. I love him more than anything. When you love someone, you need to let them be who they are. Even when it hurts. I couldn't stop him from going off to war. I can't stop him from being the hero. No one can. It's who he is."

It's who he is. Dahlia knew that. It made her heart feel too vulnerable amid an already too emotional twenty-four hours, let alone *year*. Because she just…*loved* who he was. The hero complex mixed with insecurity. The way war had marked him because he *cared*, and the way he didn't run away from any of that. The way he was with his family. The fact he couldn't soften the truth to save his life, but sometimes he wanted to, tried to.

"You might want to get used to it if you plan on sticking around," Anna added.

Before Dahlia could think of anything to say to that, a loud boom echoed through the air. The explosion shook the ground even though it seemed to come from far away.

Anna swore and took off at a run, Willie not far behind her. Dahlia stood frozen for a moment or two, but then she ran as hard as she could behind them. Toward where smoke plumed and shouts seemed to sound everywhere.

She kept sight of Willie even as Anna ran much faster than her and disappeared into the camp, but Willie, bless that dog, waited until she caught up and then took off again, leading her closer and closer to the smoke.

She could hear gunshots, but they were farther off. Was Grant involved in that? Most of the cult didn't have guns…unless like the cult from before, they'd stockpiled them somewhere.

All her thoughts stopped the moment she ran into the smoke and flickering flames of the aftermath of the explosion.

Grant was holding a kicking and screaming Rose, and Anna was trying to jump into the fray. There was shouting and shooting coming from farther off—all of it deafening—but it didn't seem to connect with whatever had happened here.

Dahlia watched as Rose fought off two people who'd done nothing but help and been nothing but kind. At her wit's end with all of it, she stepped forward.

"Stop it!" Dahlia screamed at the top of her lungs. She'd never once screamed like that in her entire life.

Rose stilled, surprisingly, and once she did, Grant took one arm and Anna the other. They were all bleeding now. All breathing hard.

"What on earth are you doing?" Dahlia demanded.

"I was going to be the sacrifice," Rose yelled right back. There were tracks of tears down her sooty cheeks. "I was going to be *chosen*. But he stopped it!" She jerked the arm Grant held, but they'd really immobilized her at this point, so she could only yank and yell in response.

Dahlia looked up at Grant. His face was also covered in black grime. He was bleeding from his lip, his nose and his temple. One of his sleeves was burned. And still he stood there stoic—the hero once again.

All the while, gunshots kept sounding in the distance. Shouting. But no more explosions, thank God.

So Dahlia focused on her sister. She stepped forward, close enough they were eye to eye. Dahlia reached out and touched her sister's cheek. "*I'm* choosing you, Rose. And life. For you."

Rose inhaled shakily, but she neither mounted an argument nor looked particularly happy.

"What do we do now?" Dahlia asked of the Hudson siblings.

"Jack's got a whole team," Anna said. "Deputies from a couple counties, some Feds, coming in from the north. Took us some time last night to track you down, but not too long. We've got an escape route to the south so we don't get caught in the…" Anna trailed off, looking first at Rose, then at Dahlia and then never finished.

Dahlia looked at her sister. Rose was staring off in the distance, her expression mutinous. But then it slowly changed, curving into a smile. Dahlia didn't trust that smile. She turned and looked at where Rose was looking while Anna was busy convincing Grant not to run toward the thick of things.

When Dahlia saw what Rose was smiling at, her heart stopped. A man standing on a hill with the perfect view of the four of them.

Holding a gun.

"Get down!" Dahlia yelled, going on instinct and tackling her sister to the ground.

Chapter Twenty-Two

It happened quickly. Dahlia yelled and dove for Rose at the same time Grant had been turning, because something had rippled up his spine. An old wartime sixth sense he'd been trying to ignore.

But Dahlia had seen it first, reacted first, and because Grant had been ignoring his instincts, he grabbed Anna just a second too late.

The gunshot went off, and his sister jerked and let out a yelp.

Grant didn't freeze. He was too well trained to freeze, but as he jumped into action to make sure they were all behind the RV and out of the shooter's target, as he checked to make sure Anna was okay, the *inside* of him froze. Even as he ordered Dahlia to keep an eye on Rose, even as Anna slapped him away and told him she was fine, he was nothing but ice.

"I'm okay," Anna said, giving him another shove with her good arm. She swore a few times, decidedly *not* proving her point. She was *bleeding*. Shot. His baby sister.

But she looked him in the eye. Fully conscious and dead serious. "It isn't bad, Grant. Look." She held up her arm. The bullet had ripped through her sleeve, and the wound bled, but he'd seen worse.

On *soldiers*. Not his baby sister.

"Your arm is burned to hell from that explosion, so don't give me any grief," Anna said.

He sucked in a breath, forcing those old war memories and deaths into the compartment they belonged in. The pain in his arm and everywhere else just seemed like old, faded memories, but Anna's comment made him understand they were real.

This was real. He was injured. And far too much was at stake. Dahlia was struggling with Rose. Trying to talk sense into her.

He didn't bother to tell Dahlia she was wasting her breath. It didn't matter. Dahlia had to do it. He understood that.

And he had to deal with the shooter. The anxiety about shooting he'd had ever since he'd been home tried to crop up. Anna was an okay shot, but she had a *wound* on her shooting arm. His burns were on his left hand.

And there was no way out if they didn't take down that shooter. And since *the gunman* kept shooting, popping one bullet against the RV after the next, Grant couldn't wait him out, hope for reinforcements and let another person get hurt.

"Give me your gun," Grant said to Anna.

She handed it over without a word. He'd done his level best to keep his shooting issues to himself, so she still thought of him as someone who could do this.

Which meant he had to.

"Don't hurt yourself, but see what you can do to help," he muttered at Anna, jutting his chin toward Rose and Dahlia's physical tussle.

"I've got four brothers. Easy peasy." She grinned at him, but she was pale and in pain and...

This had to end.

Grant took a deep breath, felt the weight of the gun and tried to block out everything else. Rose's shouts, Dahlia and Anna's earnest instructions for her to be quiet. The sound of gunfire farther off where maybe his brothers were getting themselves into a situation that—

No. Nothing else. Just taking out the gunman currently threatening him. So Anna didn't get hurt any more, and Dahlia and Rose remained as unscathed as possible.

It was up to him.

But not...*only* up to him. What he'd lost or forgotten in the military, what Dahlia had reminded him of when he'd told her about his nightmare, being honest the way his military therapist had warned him he needed to be—he was part of a family. A team. A *cog* in something bigger than himself.

Everything didn't fall on his shoulders. If it did, he'd still be in one of those tents somewhere trying to come up with a way to sneak Rose out of here against her will. He had a family, backup.

So, he only needed to take care of this one thing. And he *was* good at shooting. He *was* good at accomplishing things when he didn't let everything else crowd around and feel like only his responsibility.

He moved around the RV, calculating angles and where the shooter might be. That old calmness settled over him. When the shooter popped up the next time to fire toward the RV, Grant shot first.

He watched the man drop the gun and then tumble down the hill. He'd hit exactly where he'd meant to.

He let out a shaky breath he hadn't realized he'd been holding. He'd done it. Just like old times.

When he looked back at the women, Anna was right behind him, Dahlia having Rose somewhat subdued.

"Nice shot," Anna offered. "But you're sweating a little," she added with a grin that only trembled a *little* at the edges.

"Better than bleeding," he muttered. "Come on. Let's get the hell out of here."

GRANT AND ANNA led them away from the camp to the south so they could avoid the standoff to the north. Dahlia had to pull her sister, but Rose had stopped mounting arguments.

Granted, it probably had something to do with Anna's threat if she said one more damn word about the truth and sacrificing, Anna was going to knock her teeth out.

Yes, that hadn't been the kindest way of doing things, but it had certainly worked.

They walked for what seemed like forever, Rose walking slower and slower, her head bowing lower and lower as if each step added a weight to her back. Dahlia kept her arm firmly in Rose's but knew she couldn't reach her sister.

No one spoke, but they finally reached a small area where there were a few people milling about. There was a police cruiser and a truck. Mary rushed forward when they came into view.

"Take Anna to the hospital," Grant instructed, grabbing Anna's arm and nudging her toward Mary.

"I'm *fine*," Anna insisted. "He's the one with burns on his arm."

Mary exchanged a look with Grant over Anna's head. "Everyone else is okay?"

"Everyone here," Grant said. "Give us a few."

Mary nodded, offered Dahlia a kind smile and then took Anna toward the truck while a uniformed deputy walked over to them.

"Hey, Grant," the deputy said to him. "Ma'am," she added, nodding toward Dahlia. But when she spoke, it was to Grant. "Jack's handling up north, but he wanted me to tell you it's pretty much done. Collecting weapons, getting everyone transported. Arguing with the Feds, of course. The women will be taken to a psych eval, the men taken into whatever agencies have room. They'll sort it all out from there."

Grant nodded, then gestured at Rose. "She'll need to go with them. This is Rose Easton. The missing person Hudson Sibling Solutions has been working on."

The deputy nodded. "I can transport her myself, but I'm going to have to cuff her."

Grant looked back at Dahlia apologetically, but she understood. Much as she hated it.

"It's okay."

The deputy stepped forward, handcuffs outstretched. Rose didn't look at her, didn't mount a fight, but once the handcuffs were in place, she looked at Dahlia.

"You'll never stop the truth, Dahlia," she said. "Never."

Dahlia wanted to collapse right there, but Grant slid his arm around her shoulders as she watched her sister be lead away. "I know it seems dire," he murmured gently. "But she'll get the help she needs, and she'll be…more the woman you remember."

More. Not totally. Because no matter what help would do, Rose had been fundamentally changed in there. Just as Dahlia had been fundamentally changed trying to find her sister.

When she turned into Grant's chest, she didn't cry. But she let his gentle hold keep her upright, keep her from thinking in worst-case scenarios. He'd become…her rock. When she'd never once had one of those.

It turned out having someone to lean on was really a good thing. Because she knew, since he'd told her about his nightmare, he'd lean on her when he needed to.

But this was over, more or less, and he wasn't hers to lean on anymore. She closed her eyes and held on then for the last few moments of whatever this had been.

The next few days passed in such a blur. Dahlia didn't remember half of it. There were questions and cleanup and the Hudsons being absolute godsends.

They'd told her about cult detox programs, scholarships to pay for it. They'd driven her everywhere, taken care of everything and never once made her feel like even a second of a burden.

She supposed it was because they'd been raised

with an understanding of cults. They'd never found their missing people, but they found answers for others and had learned how to tie up all those loose ends.

Rose was still antagonistic toward Dahlia, but she was settled in a facility not far outside of Sunrise. Dahlia knew that she couldn't keep sponging off the Hudsons, but the thought of going home, of being so far from Rose, and the people who'd become her friends…

It was too much. She didn't *want* to go home. She wanted to stay put.

She just didn't know how on earth she was going to make that happen.

Opportunity came from a surprising place. Dahlia was driving her car down Main after a visit with Rose when she saw Freya on the sidewalk frantically waving at her. Dahlia pulled her car to a stop and rolled down her passenger window as Freya jogged over.

"Freya. Hi. Is everything okay?"

"Hi." Freya smiled. "Sorry to flag you down, but I wasn't sure how to get in touch in a way that I didn't have to—well, anyway." She looked up and around the street, then leaned farther into Dahlia's passenger window. "I'm leaving town."

"Oh. Well." Dahlia didn't really know what to do with this information. "I hope for good reasons?"

"Yes! I got this job at a museum in Denver,

and it's a great opportunity, and I've never been anywhere and—well, *anyway*," she said again. "My job is up for grabs. It doesn't pay much, but you seemed so taken with the library I thought I'd let you know. If you're interested, I can put in a good word for you with the library association who decides on hiring. I mean, they'd need a ré-sumé and references and all that." Freya waved it away like it was nothing.

And it was…nothing. Dahlia knew she was qualified for a small-town library position. And it would…give her the means to stay close to Rose while she completed the detox program.

And Grant.

In the days since everything had gone down, he was always there. Making sure she ate, help-ing her with logistics for Rose's care and dealing with all the legalities for both of them. Bandaged up from wounds he'd gotten helping *her*. Help-ing *Rose*.

But he'd also been…careful. And brought up her leaving often. Not because he wanted her to go, she didn't think, more like he was preparing for the eventuality.

But this was an opportunity not to have that eventuality. She smiled at Freya. "I would love if you'd put in a good word for me."

"Here." Freya handed a little card across the way. "My email and cell. Send me all your stuff. I'll get it sorted."

Dahlia looked at the card, then up at Freya. "Can I ask…why?"

Freya grinned at her. "You said the exact right thing about the library that day, and I wouldn't want to give the job to someone who didn't understand. Besides, I've been making gooey eyes at Grant almost our whole lives and I've never once seen him look at *anyone* the way he looks at you."

Dahlia felt herself blushing. "Well…"

"Just send it ASAP. You'll be a shoo-in." She stepped back from the car and offered Dahlia a little wave.

On a deep breath, Dahlia pulled away from the curb and drove to the Hudson Ranch. When she pulled up to the house, Grant was waiting for her like he always was.

Willie yipped happily and sat next to her car, tail wagging wildly while she got out. She petted him, murmuring happy greetings to him before moving on to Grant.

"You look happy," he greeted. "It went well?"

"Not really," Dahlia replied, taking the seat next to him on the porch swing. He'd made this a kind of…routine. She would get back from a visit with Rose and he and Willie would be waiting. She could talk or just sit.

He really was such a *good* man. And no matter how she told herself, or maybe it was her mother's voice in her head, that she shouldn't make decisions based on any one person…he'd saved her. And Rose. He *cared*.

He was a good man, and she was in love with him. She didn't want to go back to Minnesota, where her life had been gray and boring. She wanted to stay *here*. With Grant.

She didn't want life to be quite as exciting as it had been the past few weeks, but she wanted a life with people who made her feel like the best version of herself.

"There was no change," Dahlia said, trying to accept the bolt of pain and believe it would ease. "She still hates me and went on about truth and sacrifices."

Grant wound his arm around her shoulder. "No matter what she says, she doesn't hate you."

She didn't reply that her sister wanting her dead for any kind of truth wasn't *love*, but she understood what he meant. Rose had been psychologically traumatized and needed time. She needed healing.

She'd give Rose time and herself a life.

"I can't keep staying here, Grant. It isn't right to use your family this way." She lifted her head from his shoulder. "And don't argue with me. It is *using*."

He gave her a tight smile. "All right." He studied her face, and none of that tenseness left his expression. "But whenever you come to visit Rose, you have a place to stay. With friends." He gave her shoulder a squeeze.

And Dahlia realized she'd explained it all wrong, so she laughed.

Which caused him to frown.

"Grant, I can't leave her here." She took a deep breath and used all that bravery she'd found over the past fourteen months. She reached out and touched his cheek. "And I don't *want* to leave you."

He blew out a shaky breath, leaning his forehead to hers. "Thank *God*," he said, making her laugh. He wanted her here. Thank God, indeed.

"Freya is moving to Denver and told me she'd help get me the librarian job."

Grant pulled back a little in surprise. "Freya? Librarian job…here?"

Dahlia nodded. "She said I'd be a shoo-in. It would be a job, so I'd have income. I could find a place of my own in Sunrise. Be close enough to visit Rose and—well, to have a life. Before Rose disappeared, I wasn't really living. I was just existing. Then Rose disappeared and I was only surviving. Now I want a *life*. Here. With friends and Rose and…you."

"Good. Because that's what I want too."

She leaned forward and pressed her mouth to his, not letting herself be afraid or guilty for reveling in the *good* for once.

"I love you, Dahlia," he murmured against her mouth.

It was her turn to let out a shaky "Thank God." She looked into those steady brown eyes and smiled. "I love you too."

So, they sat on the porch talking about the future, the sound of Willie's tail thumping a happy soundtrack to the beginning of a new life.

For both of them.

* * * * *